Adeline Sergeant

Seventy Times Seven

A novel. Part 2

Adeline Sergeant

Seventy Times Seven
A novel. Part 2

ISBN/EAN: 9783337045531

Printed in Europe, USA, Canada, Australia, Japan

Cover: Foto ©Andreas Hilbeck / pixelio.de

More available books at **www.hansebooks.com**

SEVENTY TIMES SEVEN.

A Novel.

BY

ADELINE SERGEANT,

AUTHOR OF "JACOBI'S WIFE," "NO SAINT," ETC.

IN THREE VOLUMES.
VOL. II.

EDINBURGH:

OLIPHANT, ANDERSON & FERRIER.

LONDON: HAMILTON, ADAMS & CO.

1888.

CONTENTS OF VOL. II.

———◆———

SEVENTY TIMES SEVEN.

CHAPTER I.

MR. BRENDON INTERFERES.

"It's not a pleasant position," said Cecil, bending over the fire again as if he were cold, "to be engaged to one girl and in love with another."

He felt it rather a relief to disburden his mind of his troubles, even to his unsentimental younger brother.

"Is that your case?" asked Max.

"Exactly."

Max shrugged his shoulders, and reflected that Cecil must be in a bad way if he could bear to make such a confession. Nothing would have wrung from *him* so humiliating an

admission of weakness. But perhaps Max
hardly made sufficient allowance for the difference in temperament between himself and
Cecil.

"You have promised to marry one of these
Larpington girls, I suppose?"

"Larpington girls! Rather not."

"Who then?"

"Ruby Roslyn," mumbled Cecil, unwillingly.

Max did not speak for a minute. He
turned and looked at his brother with keen,
incredulous eyes and lifted brows; then, walking to the table, ostensibly to mix a second
tumbler of brandy and water, but really to
conceal the expression of his face, he said,
curtly, "I wish you joy."

"It would never have happened," said
Cecil, as if excusing his choice, "but for an
idiotic mistake on my part. I never thought
that *she* cared for me—or that I cared for her
so much——"

"And who is the 'she'?" asked Max,

deliberately dropping a lump of sugar into the tumbler, and holding it up to the light.

"She? You might know: Lenore Chaloner."

Crash!—the tumbler had somehow slipped from Max's hand, and the hot liquid was running over the carpet.

"Confound it! Why can't you remember that a fellow has nerves?" cried Cecil, angrily.

"Beg pardon: I forgot your delicate organisation," retorted Max, stooping down to pick up the broken glass. Cecil lay back in his chair, and watched the collection of the fragments and the moping up of the fragrant stream—chiefly by means of handkerchiefs.

"I don't often do a thing like that," Max said, rising with rather a pale face, as if the breakage had affected his nerves too; "but there's plenty more hot water, and I'll get another tumbler," and off he went to the pantry.

"How did you find out that she 'cared,' as you express it?" he said, on his return.

"Oh!" Cecil looked confused, "it came out : I asked her, for one thing——"

"You *asked* her!" There were volumes of reproach in Max's stern tones.

"I ought not to have done it, I know, but I had no idea that she—— What's the good of talking about it? I've half broken her heart, and the sooner I go to the devil the better."

"I don't see that that would mend matters," said Max, slowly, while Cecil covered his face with his hands and groaned by way of answer. "It's a great pity. In any case, you won't please everybody. Mother does not like Lenore, and I don't believe that the governor will consent to your marrying Miss Roslyn."

"All the better."

"The fact is that you want *him* to break it off, and then to profit by his decision, while the odium falls on him, and not on you; that's it, I suppose?"

Cecil winced, but did not reply.

"Well," said Max, after a pause, "one thing is clear. You can't marry without his consent, for you have nothing to live upon, and he will never give his consent to your marrying Ruby Roslyn. You had better make a clean breast of it to him, and perhaps he will see some way of helping you out of the scrape. I believe that he would like you to marry Lenore."

"She says that the engagement must not be broken off," said Cecil, abruptly, with his head still between his hands.

"Lenore says so? Ah, yes, *that* she would be sure to say." A wistful, almost a tender look came into Max's eyes as he proceeded. "She is a good, brave woman, candid, generous, worthy of trust and honour; you don't deserve her, and you know it. It's no good mincing the matter."

"I know it well enough; but she's my only chance," muttered Cecil. "What will become of me if I marry that—that other one?"

"Ay, that's your only cry," said Max, a little bitterly. "What will become of *me*? She's the only chance for *me*! Never a thought of what will become of *them*; and you've behaved shamefully to them both."

"If that's all the comfort you have to give me——"

"Hang it, man! don't take offence. You will have to swallow a good many hard words, I fancy, before things are put straight again. At the same time, you need not give up hope. The governor will probably take the matter entirely out of your hands; so much the better for you. Only, if he does settle it, don't change your mind again. He would not forgive a second scrape of this kind, you know. Now you must go to bed, and so must I, for I am due at the works at six."

When Cecil's aching head was laid on the pillow, Max brought him another hot draught, which he hoped would avert any dangerous consequences of his imprudence, and as he drank it the younger brother tranquilly observed :

"You need not bother your head about a formal confession of your misdeeds. I'll mention them casually to the governor to-morrow, if you like, and then you will have nothing to do but look penitent and submissive."

Cecil put out his hand impulsively, "What a good fellow you are Max !"

"Good-night," said Max, squeezing the slender white fingers extended to him, and speaking half in earnest, half in joke; "don't fall in love with a third party, while we settle which of the first two you are to marry."

But Cecil could not laugh : he turned to the wall and drew the sheet over his face with a sound suspiciously like a sob.

Max did not go to his room. He crept softly down to the library, and stood for a long time gazing into the fire with bent

brows and a somewhat pale look about his
mouth. At last he shook back his head and
shoulders, as though to rid himself of some
unpleasant thoughts, walked to the book-
case and took out a volume—it was a stiff
geometrical treatise—to which he applied
himself with a sort of dogged earnestness
until he found his eyelids growing heavy.
Then he had two hours' sleep and a bath, and
went down to his chemical works looking—to
use one of Kingsley's expressions—" as fresh
as a rose, and as dour as a door nail." Cecil
put in no appearance at breakfast time, but
his absence was too common an event to be
noticed until his brother had paid a visit to
his room and said to Mrs. Brendon, " Cecil's
not well; would you mind going to see him ? "

Mrs. Brendon hurried away, and found that
Cecil had caught a severe feverish cold.
Her presence was greatly needed at the Town
Hall, and she had the Larpingtons on her
hands; but, in spite of all her engagements

she was half disposed to stay at home and nurse him; however, the doctor laughed her fears to scorn, and said that he would be better in a day or two; and she contented herself with giving Gertrude strict orders to take care of him, and to send for her if he grew worse.

When Max went into his brother's room in the evening, Cecil turned his flushed face and languid eyes anxiously towards him, and asked a question in his hoarse voice: "Have you told him yet?"

"Not yet: I have had no chance of seeing him alone."

"You'll do it to-night?"

"If I can. It's no good precipitating matters. Now you're not to talk, you know."

"I want him to hear about it."

"Yes, yes; he'll hear quite soon enough."

"Soon enough for him, I dare say," and Cecil groaned and coughed, evidently taking it as a reproach.

"Have you heard or seen anything of Lenore?" he said, when the coughing fit was over.

"I called this afternoon, thinking you would like to know how she was. Now, if you open your lips to speak, you shall not hear a word about her." Cecil looked up with longing pathetic eyes, but said nothing. "She had been at the bazaar, but confessed to feeling tired—and looked it. She didn't say half-a-dozen words, and I did not stop five minutes."

"She did not mention me?"

"No. For goodness' sake hold your tongue."

Cecil could not forbear a smile at Max's peremptoriness, but his face soon regained its harassed expression, and though he lay still there was no ease in his posture. From these signs, as well as from his previous words, Max decided silently that the best thing he could do would be to speak to Mr. Brendon as soon

as possible. It was not an easy task to do
this, for he and his father were both unusually
busy; but the absence of Mrs. Brendon and
her daughters gave him the opportunity that
he lacked. He arranged his work so as to
have a quiet half-hour with his father in the
evening after dinner; and Mr. Brendon led
up to the subject by saying that "Cecil
seemed quite knocked up."

"No wonder," said Max, going to the point
at once; "worry always upsets Cecil."

"Worry? What's the matter with him
now?"

"Would you like a daughter-in-law,
father?"

"Eh?—Oho!"

Max could not but laugh at these two very
significant interjections, as he went on peeling
a walnut, and waited for a more definite
answer.

"I should like both of you to marry," said
Mr. Brendon, presently. "You have waited

quite long enough, I consider. Is Cecil
worrying himself about my consent?"

"Well—in one sense, yes."

"Why doesn't he come to me for it
then?"

"He is afraid the story might be a disagreeable one to you," said Max, warily.

"You mean that it is not a creditable one
to him," Mr. Brendon responded, with some
sharpness.

"I fear I am making a bad advocate," said
Max, without looking up, "so I had better
come to the point at once. Should you object
to his marrying Miss Roslyn?"

Mr. Brendon rose from his chair. "I
cannot conceive how you ask me the question.
I object decidedly; to herself, her antecedents,
her education, and everything belonging to
her. Cecil marry John Roslyn's daughter!
Not while I can prevent it." And in a white
heat of passion, Mr. Brendon walked up and
down the room, uttering threats against

Cecil, and bitter denunciations of Roslyn's dishonesty. "I tell you, Max, the man's a rogue and a swindler; he'll be in prison one of these days. No; if my son marries a Roslyn, not one penny of mine shall he ever touch."

Max waited for a pause, and struck in coolly. "That determination of yours will help Cecil out of his difficulties," he said, in a slightly satirical tone; "since he has not the faintest wish to marry Miss Roslyn—so far at least as I know."

Mr. Brendon stared. "Then what did you ask me that question for? Is it *you* who want to marry her?"

"No, thank heaven! But Cecil has had the misfortune to entangle himself in a sort of engagement with her, while at the same time he is in love with somebody else."

Mr. Brendon sat down, and looked as if he could scarcely give credit to so extraordinary a statement. His disgust found vent in a slow but emphatic exclamation. "What a fool that fellow is!" Max thought it best to eat his walnuts in silence for a few minutes, and, after some reflection, his father said sharply:

"Well, he's got himself into the mess; let him get himself out as he can. Of course, I should never sanction the engagement, but I do not see why I should be made a cat's-paw of, because he wants to marry somebody else. It's a discreditable business."

"So it is," said Max, deliberately; "but I think that somebody ought to save him from ruining himself for life. I don't believe he has the strength of will to break the engagement off, and some fine day we shall hear that Ruby Roslyn has eloped with him." A pause. "Unless we marry him out-of-hand to the girl he wants to marry."

"Who is the girl?"

"Lenore Chaloner."

"That alters the case."

"Not logically," said Max, thinking his father would be the better for a little contradiction.

"Logic has nothing to do with it."

"So it seems."

"Come now, don't you be impudent to your father, young fellow," said Mr. Brendon, whose brow had cleared wonderfully during the last few minutes. "I should like to hear when Cecil told you this fine story?"

"Late last night. He had a sort of explanation with Lenore—a silly thing to do, it seems to me—and found out that she liked him, and was very tragic over it, you know. There has been a nasty complication; first, he made love to Lenore, then to Ruby, and now——"

"And now to both of them at once. It appears to me," said Mr. Brendon, "that he has acted very dishonourably in the matter."

"He has been weak, not wilfully wicked. A good wife would be the saving of him."

"Perhaps. I don't know. I think Lenore Chaloner is too good for him."

"We shall have to be careful about Lenore's feelings. She says that Cecil must fulfil his engagement to Ruby; and unless *you* break it off, father, not Cecil, I don't believe she will have anything to do with him."

"She is a good girl," said Mr. Brendon, thoughtfully. "I should like Cecil to marry her, though I don't suppose his mother will approve. I must think over the matter. Cecil knows that you are telling me, I conclude?"

"He was very anxious that I should do so. He was going to tell you himself, but I offered to talk it over with you first, because I— thought——"

"Thought what?"

Max temporised. "Well, sir, Cecil's a trifle afraid of you when you are angry. Don't you know how difficult it is to him to tell you anything that he thinks you will not like?"

"He should not do things I don't like, then. Well, well! perhaps it was better that I had not got him here to blow up, for the idea of his marrying that girl made me very angry. In fact, I am very angry now."

"Draw it mild with him, won't you, sir?" said Max, a trifle more eagerly than usual. "He is really suffering for his imprudence."

"I don't call it imprudence," observed the father; "I call it dishonourable folly and meanness, and I intend to tell him so. Stuff, Max; leave him to me. He does not deserve Lenore if he can't see that he has treated her badly."

"He does see that."

"All right; I hope he does. Nay, if he gets me to do what he wants, he must take a bit of my mind as well."

And Max was obliged to be content, although he would fain have had a fuller assurance that his father was not going to be hard on Cecil.

The following day was a particularly busy one, and he had time only to snatch his meals at home, and could not exchange two words with his brother until evening. About six he looked into Cecil's room, and found his father standing by the fire. He would have retired, but Mr. Brendon called out to him to come in. Cecil was lying back on his pillows, the feverish crimson of his cheeks and the brilliance of his dark eyes making him look hardly fit for any fresh excitement. He had always been subject to these attacks of severe cold and low fever, and the present illness was unusually prostrating.

"Yes," Mr. Brendon was saying as Max came in, "I can't say that I think your conduct has been honourable, or even creditable."

Cecil tried to speak, but his voice was nearly gone, and he could only look half-appealingly at Max, who said gruffly,

" Cecil ought not to talk, even to say so.'

"I don't want him to talk," said Mr. Brendon. "I have only required him so far to listen to me. I have been telling him that I shall not consent to his engagement with Miss Roslyn, and I have already been down to her father and said so. That matter is virtually at an end. Miss Roslyn is to send back your ring and other fine presents to-morrow. After this folly, Cecil, the sooner you make a sensible marriage the better. That is all I wish to say just now. The sooner you get well, the sooner we can put these affairs into right order."

Cecil managed to croak out the observation that he was sorry that he had not pleased his father.

"Sorry? I daresay. People are generally sorry — afterwards — when they have made fools of themselves," was Mr. Brendon's grim reply. "However, least said soonest mended. I do not want to reproach you either for your conduct to Miss Roslyn or to Miss Chaloner,

but to get you out of your present embarrass-
ing position.   When you assume the duties of
a married man, I hope you will learn more
wisdom than you appear to possess at present.
That's enough of the subject.—Your cold
doesn't seem much better."

"He's feverish," said Max, "and wants to
be kept quiet."

"And who prevents his being quiet ?   You
mean me, I presume," said his father, between
anger and amusement.   "Well, all I can do
is to let him alone, then.   Good-night, Cecil,"
and he went up to the bed and took his son's
hot hand, not unmindful of the tears that
sprang, chiefly from bodily weakness, to
Cecil's eyes as he did so.   "Don't agitate
your mind over this business ; I'll see you
well out of it.   And you may give some
credit to your brother there.   But for him,
I should never have moved hand or foot in
the matter, I can tell you.   I hope you'll
have a better night."

Cecil could do little talking, but he was right in telling himself, if he could tell nobody else, that father and brother treated him more leniently than he deserved. He was relieved to find that Mr. Brendon would not sanction the engagement, and yet was secretly ashamed of himself when he acknowledged that his father's commands would have had little weight with him had he *wished* to keep faith with Ruby.

His presents to Miss Roslyn came back to him next morning without a word of expostulation or farewell.

CHAPTER II.

THE settlement of Cecil's affairs did not give
Max much satisfaction. He thought, rightly
enough, that his brother's conduct had been
inexcusable; and there appeared to him something mean in the way in which Cecil
sheltered himself behind his father's disap-
proval as a means of ridding himself of the
woman to whom he had "made love" without
serious intention of marriage. Cecil's illness,
as well as something inherently lovable in his
nature, made Max less hard upon him than he
would have been on any other man under the
same circumstances; at the same time, he could
not refrain from uttering a few severe comments
on the matter, even while he was inter-

22

ceding with his father on Cecil's behalf, and smoothing Cecil's path for a reconciliation with Lenore.

It had been a shock to him to find that Cecil's heart was really given to Lenore Chaloner. In old days he had certainly thought that such was the fact; but during the last three months he had believed, as everybody else had believed, that Cecil was thinking no more of her. He had wondered whether Lenore grieved over Cecil's desertion —for desertion indeed it seemed; and it was this doubt that had made him think more seriously than ever of the possibility of asking Lenore to be his wife. On reviewing the past, he could not easily tell why he had not already done so. The last thing that he would have acknowledged was that any other woman had touched his heart more deeply than Lenore; and yet if he had been a more sentimental man, or more accustomed to observe the workings of his own mind, he

would have noticed that it was not Lenore
of whom he thought most frequently, not
Lenore whose opinion of his actions was im-
portant to him, not Lenore whose face hovered
before him in his dreams and in the silent
watches of the night. But the last thing that
occurred to him was that he could be in love
with Magdalen Lingard.

He cared for Lenore very much, but in a
brotherly, protecting way. The pain that
Cecil's revelation gave him was caused by
sorrow for her, not for himself. He foresaw
unhappiness for her, whether she married Cecil
or whether she did not, and he was grieved to
think of his brother's unworthiness. It was
natural that he should mistake this feeling for
that of love—the sober, rational kind of love
in which he believed—and half persuade
himself that he was suffering for the loss of
Lenore, and that henceforth he must put the
idea of marriage out of his mind.

He went to see Lenore, however; diffidently,

at first, afterwards with increasing satisfaction. He found that he did not suffer quite so much as he had expected, although he kept himself well in mind of the fact that she would some day be his sister-in-law, and not his wife. In a very short time, indeed, he had almost forgotten to suffer at all, and thought with complacency of the time when Cecil should make a home for himself, and when he—Max —would be always welcome at the house— first as the bachelor brother; afterwards, perhaps, as the bachelor uncle to Cecil's boys and girls. Max found himself thinking quite cheerfully of this prospect, and began to understand that his love-trouble had not gone very deep.

But as yet the day of Cecil's marriage with Lenore seemed far distant. It was evident that she had been bitterly hurt by Cecil's treatment of her, and that she took Max's view of his behaviour towards Ruby Roslyn. She would not allow any one to mention the

subject to her; she talked of other things if
Cecil's name were mentioned at her grandmother's table; she steadily refused all invitations to the Brendons' house.   Plainly it would
be a hard matter to win her back to him, and
Max sometimes wondered whether Cecil would
succeed in his enterprise.   He was not very
certain of his brother's steadiness of purpose.

The illness that had assailed Cecil at this
conjuncture was undoubtedly a fortunate turn
in his affairs.   It was not exactly a serious
attack, but by it he was secluded in his own
room, safely out of reach of sneers from his
old companions: safe, too, from the displeasure of his father and the surprise of his
sisters; or at any rate from absolute expression of it, for his sisters had no heart to
reopen wounds from which he was suffering so
severely.   Of course Gertrude and Ursula
somewhat misunderstood the cause of his
depression, fancying that he had really cared
for Ruby, and was grieving over an enforced

separation from her; and this misunder-
standing added to the usual coldness of
Ursula's manner towards him, because, in her
opinion, he ought to have been constant to
the woman that he loved, instead of tamely
relinquishing her at a word from his father.
Mr. Brendon, too, could not repress an
occasional dryness of tone or severity of
phrase towards him. He was much vexed to
find that Cecil could behave so foolishly and
so dishonourably. "He had always thought
him a bit of a fool," the father did not scruple
to say in the first moments of his anger, " but
he had had no idea that the lad was a scoun-
drel, too." Mrs. Brendon, on the other hand,
declared that poor Cecil had not been to
blame. That artful girl had entrapped him,
and he was quite right to get free from her at
any cost. Thus, though everybody who came
into contact with him considered that he was
very tenderly treated, Cecil was not without
thorns in his pillow; and conscience and

imagination supplied voice to the reproaches
which nobody uttered in words.   Max was
the most agreeable person in the household
to him, because Max did not say soft things
in order to pacify his mind; and if he thought
that his brother had acted "like a born idiot,"
did not mind telling him so, whether he had a
cold on his chest or not.

Cecil's recovery was a tedious affair.   The
low fever hung about him till he was much
weaker than he ought to have been from so
apparently trivial an illness.   His unquiet-
ness of mind retarded his improvement.
Nobody knew how he hungered and thirsted
for Lenore.   If she had asked after him, or
sent any message, he felt as though he could
have borne his humiliation of spirit; but she
let her grandmother do all the questioning
when Max called, and, while really listening
attentively to his answers, never gave the
faintest sign of interest in them.   In fact,
though the effort of self-control was sometimes

almost more than she could bear, she acted perfect indifference with such success that Max was startled into the conviction that Cecil's suit was hopeless, and that he would never be forgiven.

Touched by Cecil's restless misery, Max at last persuaded his father to go to Lenore and ask her to take a little pity on the sick man. But Lenore would not be persuaded. She declined to pay Cecil a visit, or to promise forgiveness of any kind.

"She's a hard-hearted little thing, although she looks so frail," Mr. Brendon said afterwards to Max, in a burst of confidence, "and I believe that Cecil has just fooled away all his chances with her. However, we had better leave her alone now. When Cecil is well enough to plead his own cause, perhaps she will relent. I don't know why *I* should mix myself up with these boy and girl love-affairs," he added, in a tone of offence, at which Max laughed heartily.

Max had also a cause for anxiety of which he could not rid himself. His friend and favourite, James Lloyd, had recovered from his accident and returned to the office. His manner was a little graver than usual, but he had worked well, and been as simple and kindly in his ways as ever until the beginning of Cecil's illness, and the rupture of that unacknowledged engagement between Cecil and Ruby Roslyn. Then, Max noticed, his manner began to change.

It was impossible to suppose that he did not know part, at least, of the story. The Roslyns had not been reticent on the subject. Ruby herself might perhaps have held her tongue; but her father, her brother, and her sisters were very bitter against Mr. Brendon and his sons. Mr. Roslyn raved about " breach of promise " cases; and Ted Roslyn threatened to horsewhip any man who behaved shabbily to his sister—a vague threat which did not bode great harm to anybody.

For, after all, it was not Cecil who had re-
nounced Ruby; Mr. Brendon had taken all
the responsibility on himself, and simply for-
bidden the marriage. He, Max, and Lenore
were the only persons who knew the true
state of Cecil's feelings. But did Ruby sus-
pect it? And had she told James Lloyd of
her suspicions? Else, why should his brow
have become gloomy, and why should his
eye be so pertinaciously averted when Max
spoke to him? This period of gloom and
depression lasted a few days, and then Mr.
Brendon informed his son that young Lloyd
had thrown up his situation and was coming
to the office no more.

" What's that for?" said Max.

" Don't know, I am sure. I heard some
rumour of his mother's marrying again; perhaps that has something to do with it."

" I'll go round and find out. We shall
miss him."

" I'm not sure that I would have him back

here, even if he changed his mind. I can't
have any shilly-shallying."

"But there was no unpleasantness? nothing wrong?"

"Oh no, nothing. I don't know in the
least why he wants to leave. I have not had
time to inquire."

"You would not mind my taking him on
at the Works, if he would come, I suppose?"
said Max, who saw a glimmer of reason for
Lloyd's departure from a place where Cecil
would perhaps be master by and bye.

"Of course not; do as you like about that."

Max made his way to Mrs. Lloyd's house
as soon as he had an hour to spare, but was
told that James was not at home. One of the
younger children opened the door and answered his questions with such a frightened
air that Max's suspicions were aroused. "Is
your mother in?" he asked.

"No—yes—I don't know," said the child,
looking round, as if for help.

' Go and see," said Max, good-humouredly. " I will wait until you come back."

The child hurriedly decamped ; and Max, who had always made himself at home at the Lloyds', walked coolly into the passage and opened the little parlour door. There he stood for a moment amazed. The room seemed full of guests, to his unaccustomed eyes. Then he took off his hat, said formally, " I beg your pardon," and returned to the hall, shutting the door behind him.

Mrs. Lloyd, James Lloyd, and Ruby Roslyn were in the little parlour, and Ruby was sobbing as if her heart would break.

Max walked straight to the front-door, and would have gone out never to enter it again, had not Mrs. Lloyd pursued him. She also shut the door carefully behind her, thus, as Max noticed, leaving James and Ruby alone together.

" Mr. Max, oh, Mr. Max," she exclaimed,

nervously, "please wait just one moment. I'm so sorry—I hope you won't go away, sir; I hope you're not vexed."

Probably the sternness of the face that he now turned upon her had something to do with her last words.

"I don't think you need have made your little girl tell lies about it," he said. "If you did not want me to come in, you might have said so."

Mrs. Lloyd at once dissolved into tears. "I'm very sorry, sir," she said. "I didn't mean it; but Miss Roslyn was there, and Jim didn't want to say——"

"It's of no consequence; I can see Jim another time," Max answered, still somewhat curtly; but Mrs. Lloyd would not let him go without further explanations.

"We didn't know that it was you, Mr. Max. We wanted to keep the gossiping neighbours out, and that was all. For they *will* talk, and I'm sure it doesn't matter to them if the poor

.girl likes to drop in now and then, and talk over her troubles——"

The murder was out. Mrs. Lloyd stopped short, remembering to whom she spoke. But Max did not look angry now, only thoughtful and attentive.

" Does she come often ?" he asked, quietly.

" Oh, not so very often," said Mrs. Lloyd, twisting her watch-guard nervously between her fingers; "just now and then when she wants a little sympathy, because it's a bit hard for her at home just now——"

" Does she come to Jim for sympathy ?"

" Well, Jim was always fond of her," answered Mrs. Lloyd, whose tone had changed considerably since Max last conversed with her on the subject, " and if she gets any good out of a talk with him, I don't see why she shouldn't have it, poor thing !"

The two were standing on the door-step, where the darkness of night was already beginning to envelop them. Suddenly the

parlour-door opened, and a figure emerged
from the inner room. It was Ruby, cloaked
and veiled almost beyond recognition. She
said no word to Mrs. Lloyd, but dashed
between her and Max, down the path and out
at the gate, without a moment's pause.

There was a little silence. Then Max—still
watching the dark figure before it disappeared
into the night—said quietly,

" Will James see me now ? "

Mrs. Lloyd went back to the parlour. Max
could not help hearing a few words of the
colloquy that followed. " Why should he
come ? . . . Don't want any interfering. . . .
Had enough of the Brendons for one while."
Such were some of the phrases that fell
upon his ear, in tones that were not those
of the Jim Lloyd that Max used to know.
Mrs. Lloyd's words were indistinguishable :
from the pleading, piteous accents, Max
imagined, however, that she was begging her
son to receive the visitor.

Max would be put off no longer. He stepped once more to the parlour door. "It's the first time you have ever refused to see me, Jim," he said.

Silence fell upon the wrangling tongues. In the dark little room the three figures stood motionless for a moment. Then Jim turned away.

"You can come in if you like, sir," he said, almost sullenly. "I don't know what you can have to say to me, that is all. Mother, will you light the gas?"

Mrs. Lloyd did as she was desired, with trembling fingers; then let down the blind and hurried out of the room. She was afraid of something that she saw in her son's face.

The two young men stood on opposite sides of the centre table, facing one another. A stronger contrast scarcely could have been presented between any two men of the same race, and of nearly the same age. One was broad-shouldered, dark, sturdy, with a look

of vigorous health of body and of mind ; the
other, fair, slight, with sloping shoulders and
slender frame, his blue eyes bright with a
febrile excitement which he laboured unsuccessfully to conceal. Max was shocked by the
change in his manner and appearance. The
young man's face was flushed, his brow lower-
ing ; as Max looked at him steadily, he turned
away, and leaned with his arm on the
mantelpiece. Something was evidently very
wrong.

"What's all this about, Jim ?" said Max,
using the old friendly voice that was natural
to him, but eyeing Lloyd very keenly all the
time.

"All what, sir ?" The tone was dogged
and sullen ; Jim's pliant gentleness of manner
had disappeared.

"Well—why have you left my father's
office ?"

"I don't know that that's any one's business
but my own, sir."

"True enough.   But a friend has a right to ask a question when he sees a man throwing away a good chance in life."

Jim's pale face flushed more deeply than ever, and the blue veins upon his forehead began to swell.

"There are as good chances on the other side of the water as there are here, I suppose," he said, defiantly.

"Yes, if you have introductions.   I don't know that you will find it easier to get on in New York or Philadelphia without them than you would in Scarsfield or London.   However, there's a man I know in New York; I shall be pleased to write to him about you if you think of going there.   Unless, of course, you have been offered a berth already."

Jim shook his head.

"You mean it kindly, I dare say," he responded, with some abatement of the roughness of his manner, "but you don't understand.   I'll make my own way without

introductions. I shall get work, I have no
doubt."

"At the docks or the wharves, perhaps,"
said Max, rather sharply, "where your
strength will break down in a week's time.
Men of your physique can't do that sort of
work, Jim. And what will become of your
mother?"

"Mother's provided for," said Lloyd, with
a short laugh. "She's going to marry
Bracy, the joiner, who says he'll support the
children as well as herself. I am free to do
what I choose."

"And is there no other way of using your
freedom but cutting yourself off from your
friends and doing work that will kill you in a
few days or weeks? If you want to leave
Scarsfield, do it in a rational way. Let me
write to Mr. Brownlow in New York——"

"It's no use," said Jim, removing his elbow
from the mantelpiece, and for the first time
looking Max fairly in the face. "As I said

before, you don't understand—or you *won't*
understand, which is perhaps more likely—
you *won't* understand that I would rather
starve in the streets than take a penny-piece
from any one of your family again. I should
be ashamed to do it, and so I tell you to your
face. You rich folks think that the poor have
no feelings, no honour, no dignity. I'm a
poor man myself, but I would die rather than
act as your brother has acted to a girl that
loved him. And not only your brother, but
your father and yourself! What consideration
had you for her? what pity? what generosity?
Wasn't she as good as you? She was good
enough to be made love to by Mr. Cecil
Brendon; good enough to play with, and then
to cast aside! I'll have no more to do with
any of the lot of you; and I take it as an
insult that you should ask me why, when you
know that she's the woman that I love—
the woman that I should be proud to call
my wife!"

CHAPTER III.

MAX listened very quietly to this tirade.
When Jim had finished, and stood before him
with flushed face and quivering lips, the hand
with which he had struck the table more than
once during his speech still trembling with
agitation, the elder man asked a question that
fell like ice on the young fellow's heated spirit.

"Have you taken leave of your senses,
Jim ?"

"That's always the way!" cried Lloyd,
turning away and striking his hand upon the
the little painted mantelpiece; "that's always
the way! If a man shows any honest indignation against a wrong, you say that he's out
of his senses!"

42

"I think that you must be out of your senses, certainly, to apply such words either to my father or to myself," said Max steadily. "You know well enough that we can feel indignation against wrong-doing. As to my brother—now, look here, James Lloyd, I will speak frankly. My brother has been exceedingly foolish and weak, I grant you that, but he has not done anything that *you* have a right to call him in question for. He and Miss Roslyn had an understanding between themselves; that was no business of yours. He told his father of the engagement, and his father objected to it, and threatened to cut off the supplies unless he gave it up. Well, he yielded; what else could he do under the circumstances?"

"He could have taken his own way, and worked for a living like an honest man!" said James Lloyd, impetuously.

"That would have meant struggle and poverty. Would that sort of life suit Miss

Roslyn, do you think? I am quite sure that
it would not suit my brother. He is in very
delicate health."

"I call it the act of a coward to give up the
woman you love at a father's command," said
Lloyd, in a somewhat grandiloquent manner.
His sentences grew curter and more pointed as
he went on. "But that wasn't the case. He
did not love her. He wanted to get rid of her.
It was he who grew tired first. He's broken
her heart."

"My good fellow, hearts are not so easily
broken," said Max, a little out of countenance.
Had Jim guessed all this, or was it Ruby who
put him on this tack?

Lloyd saw the impression that he had produced, and continued with increasing vehemence.

"*She* knows how it came about, if nobody
else does. He likes somebody else. And in
order to get him out of the scrape, you and
your father put your heads together to devise

a way of preventing the marriage. Her father's reputation, her position, the quarrel between Mr. Roslyn and Mr. Brendon—I know the whole story."

"Scarcely," said Max. "I don't wish to maintain that my brother has acted with great courage or spirit, but I do maintain that he did not break off the engagement with Miss Roslyn until he was forced to do so by his father. And I must say too that I don't think Miss Roslyn would have made a good wife for him. On that ground I too was against the marriage."

"I knew you were—I knew it. *She* told me so. She said that Mr. Brendon said so. I never should have thought that you would have helped your brother to do such a dastardly thing!"

The impressible young fellow's emotion was changing its character. The tears were near his eyes as he spoke, and he put up his hand to rub them away.

"My dear Jim," said Max, kindly, "nobody can have been more sorry about the matter than I. But I don't see that either you or I could have done anything to stay the course of events; and still less do I see why you should throw up your position and means of livelihood in this country from some Quixotic notion about not taking money from our family. I can understand that you mayn't care to work under Cecil any longer; if so, come to me. I should like to have you down at the Caustic Works, I want a fellow of your capacity."

Jim shook his head: his face was very pale.

"No, Mr. Max, I couldn't do it—unless ——"

"Unless what?"

"Unless Mr. Cecil were to marry Miss Roslyn straight away——"

"Against his father's wishes?"

"Yes. If he'll brave the world for her I'll forgive him everything."

" You know that that's impossible."

". Then it's impossible for me to serve any member of your family, sir. You yourself will be the first to say that it's impossible, by and bye."

"Why, what do you mean?" asked Max, struck by something indescribably ominous in the tone. "Why should it be more impossible by and bye than it is now?"

" Because he'll have one more chance to do the right thing; and if he refuses, then—let him look out."

" Do you mean that for a threat?"

" Never mind what I mean, Mr. Max. I've no wish to quarrel with you. I beg your pardon if I've said hasty words about your conduct. I know that it's only natural that you should side with your family."

" James," said Max, very seriously, "if you are contemplating—as I can hardly believe that you are mad enough to contemplate— any scheme of—of—revenge——"

The young fellow burst out laughing. The laugh was an odd one, hard and forced, and with it the glitter came back to his large blue eyes.

"Revenge?" he said, with scornful emphasis. "Revenge? Its right name would be punishment." Then he turned round to the mantelpiece again and stood with his head leaning on his folded arms, heedless of any further remark that Max addressed to him.

Max took the trouble to treat the matter very seriously, to argue, even to plead with him, concerning his wild speeches. But it was apparently labour thrown away. Jim would respond neither by look nor word. Max quitted the house at last, sorrowfully aware that he had failed to make an impression, and hoping only that his words would sink into the hearer's mind by degrees, and gradually produce some result.

He thought chiefly, however, about the effect of the whole affair on James Lloyd's mind. He did not believe that any harm would come of that half-implied threat, that talk of revenge or punishment. Lloyd had hitherto seemed such a gentle-natured fellow, that it was difficult to realise the depth of the passions that possessed him. Max recalled a half-forgotten story of Lloyd's relations; two, if not three, of them had surely gone out of their minds, and ended their lives either by suicide or in a lunatic asylum. Was there, some hereditary taint in the poor lad's blood? some weakness of brain that excitement might turn to lunacy? Max trusted not; yet felt that were it so, the poor fellow's bitter rage might more easily be forgiven.

He gave Cecil a warning of possible danger, in a somewhat vague way, for he did not want to mention James Lloyd's name; but Cecil seemed supremely indifferent to the matter. His health was beginning to return; and a new spring of hope was rising within his breast.

Christmas Day and New Year's Day had passed before Cecil was able to venture forth from the house. Fortunately for him it was a mild January, and his strength grew apace in the soft, cloudy weather, which was almost like that of spring. Max began to lose his fears concerning him. Nothing more was heard of Ruby Roslyn, nothing of James Lloyd; Lenore had relaxed her severity of demeanour, and although she would not yet acknowledge that she had forgiven her recreant lover, there seemed good hope of her doing so before very long. Everything was going well when Cecil, by the fatal weakness which belonged to his character, again brought down misfortune on his own head.

He was sitting in the library one morning and thinking languidly that he would venture to call upon Miss Chaloner before another day had passed, when a note was handed to him. He changed colour as he saw the hand-writing. It was that of Ruby Roslyn.

"Father wants me to go away from Scarsfield for a time, but I must see you once
before I go. Don't say no. It shall be for
the last time.—R. R."

So ran the note.

Cecil temporised. He wrote back, saying
that there was no place in which they could
possibly meet, their respective homes being
least available of all places for that purpose.
Ruby's reply was ready:

"I hear that you have been out walking
several times. You might meet me on the
Quay, at the end of Orwell Lane, about six
o'clock this evening. I shall be there."

Cecil wavered, cursed his ill-luck, and
decided to go. That he was running a risk he
knew well enough; six o'clock on a January
evening was the worst possible time for him
to make an excursion of the kind, but he had
a weak and foolish feeling that he owed Ruby
the interview that she desired. It was a
difficult thing to escape from the vigilance of

his family, but he accomplished this feat by
dint of a little insincerity, and repaired to the
Quay at the appointed time.

The place was an odd one for such a meeting. The stone piers and docks that skirted
the river for some distance presented a very
desolate appearance when the tide was down,
for only when the tide was at its height
could much business be transacted. When
Cecil repaired thither the quays were nearly
deserted; one or two men sat smoking on
barges in the basins, and the farthermost pier
of all, stretching far out into the river, was
completely empty. Here Cecil encountered
Ruby, and, almost without speaking, they
proceeded towards its most retired corner,
which was hidden from the view even of
ordinary wayfarers by a round tower, occasionally tenanted by a coastguardsman. Ruby
was dressed with unusual plainness, and wore
a thick veil; perhaps with unnecessary assumption of mystery, but at any rate with an

eye to the becoming. When she let the black
gauze fly back over her picturesque hat from
her brilliantly-tinted dark face, and showed
herself dressed in the very darkest of plain
dark dresses, Cecil knew instinctively that she
had never looked so well. He felt himself at
a disadvantage; he was already languid and
fatigued by the walk, and the cool breeze
made him shiver, and robbed him of his voice.
There was some new softness in Ruby's eyes,
some new timidity in her manner, which
tended to make Cecil more uncomfortable
than he had expected to be. He had
laboured, not unsuccessfully, to believe that
Ruby's heart had never really been touched,
that only her vanity and her ambition were
excited by his flirtation (for so he called it)
with her, and that of the two, he had suffered
more than she. Believing all this, it was
inexplicable and disconcerting to him to see
this change in her manner—a change that
told of deeper feeling and stronger passion

than had ever been associated with his ideas
of Ruby Roslyn.

He did not see—and Ruby did not see—
that another figure was hovering near.   A
man had followed the girl as she came down
Orwell Lane; he had tracked her footsteps
along the quay, and had now slipped into a
little niche in the stonework of the tower,
where he could lie concealed in the shadows,
within hearing of every word that was spoken.
If Cecil could have seen that crouching figure,
if he could have distinguished in the darkness
the threatening expression of those sullen,
watchful eyes, he might well have weighed his
words.   As it was, he feared nothing but an
explosion of wrath from Ruby, and wished the
interview well over.

"I wanted to see you once more," she said,
laying her ungloved hand on Cecil's arm.
"Just once; you don't mind, do you?"

"Mind! Of course not.   I am only too
glad to see you again," he answered—unable,

for the life of him, to speak sincerely, when a woman's pleading eyes were fixed upon his face.

"Is it true, Cecil? Must it all be at an end?" she asked.

He turned away from her and spoke sharply.

"Why on earth do you want to give me the pain of saying it? I can't help myself—I'm the most miserable dog alive!" And at that moment he certainly was sincere.

Ruby burst into tears.

"It does give you pain, then?" she sobbed. "You do care? It isn't true what father has been saying, that you are only too glad to get rid of me, and that you want to marry somebody else?—It isn't true?"

Cecil stood silent, with downcast eyes. He could not bring himself, with the thought of Lenore in his mind, actually to tell a lie.

"Our engagement is at an end," he said, after a pause. "What is the use of talking

about it now ?   We could not marry without
an income ; we are in exactly the same position, you and I ; we can do nothing without
the consent of our parents.   We are helpless
in the matter."

She pressed closer to him, her eyes shining
through her tears.

" But if we were free, Cecil ?—if you had
some money of your own ?   You do care for
me a little, don't you ? "

" I—I care for you very much, Ruby ; I
care for your happiness and your welfare,"
said Cecil, faltering.

" Fathers don't live for ever," said the girl,
quite unconscious, in her eagerness, of the
thrill of repulsion that ran through Cecil's
whole frame as she spoke, "and our day
might come yet, if only you would wait for
me as I would wait for you.   I 'd wait a life-
time, Cecil.   But perhaps you—you—you 've
changed ? "

Cecil turned away his face.

"We should never be happy together, Ruby," he said, trying to pluck up a little courage, but not daring to meet her eager glance. "We are too different—different in our aims, our lives; different in every way. Love would not be sufficient to disguise this difference—even from ourselves. Perhaps it is that we do not love each other enough."

"Speak for yourself!" cried Ruby, in her impetuous, outspoken way. "I——"

She suddenly stopped short. A deep crimson flush rose to her cheeks and forehead; a new look came into her eyes. She began to feel, almost for the first time, that she was forcing her love upon a man who did not care for it. Her womanly instincts had never been much cultivated, but just now they leaped into sudden life.

"You mean," she said, in an altered tone, "that father was right?—that I've been mistaken after all?" Her lip trembled, but her sobs had ceased, though the tears still lingered on her hot cheek. Cecil leaned his elbows on the narrow stone parapet, and covered his face with his hands, saying nothing. The girl's eyes began to flame.

"I see," she said. "I was wrong, then. I thought—well, it doesn't matter what I thought. Who's cut me out? I've a right to know that, at any rate. Who is she?"

Lenore's name fell reluctantly from Cecil's lips. It seemed to him that, as Ruby said, she had a right to know.

"I knew her before I knew you," he pleaded by way of excuse. "I had made her love me—she had a claim on me——" And then, by one of his many contradictory impulses, he took a manlier tone. "I won't say that. I mean that I loved her all along. I thought that she did not care for me, and so I tried to forget her. But I shall never forget her; I love her with my whole heart, and no one else."

n his desire to be explicit, Cecil was almost

cruel—as weak men are apt to be. Struck by
the look of pain upon her face, he came closer
to her side, and tried to take her hand. Now
that the decisive words had been spoken, he
felt brave.

" Don't touch me ! " she said, starting back
from him. " Don't come near me ! I hate
you—I despise you ! "

" I am deeply ashamed of my conduct,
Ruby," said Cecil.

" So you should be. But you 're not ; I
know you 're not. You are thinking how soon
you can get away from me and go back to
Lenore—Lenore ! that insignificant, pale-faced
chit ! Well, go to her and forget me, forget
me as soon as you can, and I 'll forget you too.
But no, no, I shan't forget you, that is the
worst of it ; " and the girl's voice rose plain-
tively on the still night air—" I shall never,
never forget."

She hid her face in her hands, and stood
motionless for a moment, as if trying to realise

the extent of her despair. Cecil, dismayed by
her vehemence, murmured some words of
commonplace consolation. He did not see,
and she also did not see, the baleful glitter of
the eyes that watched him from that secret
lurking-place ; he could not in the gloom distinguish the look of set purpose on the
watcher's features, or the threatening gesture
of the watcher's hand. At that moment he
went in peril of his life, and knew it not.

"Forgive me," he murmured, more humbly
than he had spoken yet. "It is no use to
say that I am sorry, but I do grieve deeply,
Ruby, I——"

"Oh, for pity's sake stop !" she cried, fling-
ing her hands away from her face with a
gesture of passionate despair. "Do you think
I care whether you are sorry or not ? What
good will your sorrow do ? You have broken
my heart, that's all."

And with a cry more like that of a wounded
animal than a human being, she sped away

from him into the gathering shadows of the night.

Cecil gathered himself up to follow her, but his strength was not yet very great, and he was ashamed and astonished to find himself shaking from head to foot, dizzy and sick, as if he had received a blow. Before he could master himself sufficiently to advance more than a few steps, she was out of sight. He paused again and strained his eyes to catch some glimpse of her, but she was nowhere to be seen. Probably she had gone home; it was no use to follow her.

He straightened himself up and drew a long breath of relief. "Thank heaven, *that's* over!" he muttered, half aloud to himself. He had no thought of being overheard, and started violently when a low stern voice fell upon his ear, and a fierce grip was laid upon his arm.

"It's not over yet," said the voice. "You've got to smart for what you have done,

Cecil Brendon.   She said that you had broken
her heart, and, by God, if you have, you shall
pay for it."

Cecil heard no more.   A hail of crushing
blows about his head and shoulders had
brought him to his knees; once and again the
heavy stick descended, then he fell forward
upon his face and lay quite still.

Ruby's wrongs had been avenged.

CHAPTER IV.

"MY WIFE!"

MAX BRENDON came out of his father's house one evening with bent brow and anxious eyes, from which it seemed as if sleep had been banished for more than one long and weary night. He did not look up as he walked along the garden-path, but it was evident that his mind was occupied with a settled purpose, for he went straight to the gate of the little Red House, and knocked with a peculiarly resolute air at the Red House door.

Lenore saw him come. Her grandmother was out; indeed, she and the maid-servant were alone together in the house. Max was ushered as usual into the little front sitting-room, where he found the girl standing near

the centre-table in an expectant attitude.
She looked as if she longed yet dreaded to see
him enter. Her hands were clasped tightly
together; her eyes were strained and anxious,
her lips white. Max went up to her and held
out his hand; she put her trembling fingers
into it and looked piteously up into his grave
face, but she could not speak.

"I have come to tell you how he is to-
night," Max said, letting his eyes rest upon
her fair face with pity and tenderness. If
ever he had thought of Lenore as other than
a sister, he had forgotten it : now and hence-
forward she was to him simply the woman
that his brother loved, dear for his sake,
almost as dear as Ursula herself. The grave
sympathy of his voice and eyes gave her
courage. She faltered out a question.

"He is no worse ?"

"No, we think not. The doctor thinks that
he is no worse."

"Oh, thank God!" She drew her hand

hurriedly away, and covered her eyes with it,
turning from Max a little, so as, if possible,
to hide the rush of involuntary tears. He
remained silent for a moment or two, and
when she was calmer she began to excuse
herself for her show of emotion.

"I did not mean to be so foolish," she said,
" but you know how anxious we have all been
during the last three days ! And now that he
is better——"

"I am afraid," said Max, reluctantly, "that
I did not say that he was *better*; only no
worse."

She caught her breath. "Only no worse !"

" Since he was found insensible on the Quay
and carried home, you know that he has been
in a sort of stupor. The blows upon the head
must have caused some injury to the brain;
and now he is delirious. The doctors want
him to be kept as quiet and calm as possible;
it is his only chance of recovery. Lenore, he
constantly calls for you."

" For me ? " She listened, with her eyes fixed intently on Max's face.

" For you. He wants you to go to him. The doctors say that your presence might calm him. Will you come ? "

She did not hesitate, though her face grew pale and her hands began to tremble. " Oh, take me to him ; take me to him now," she said. " Why do you stay so long ? "

Max gently detained her. "A few minutes' delay will make no difference," he said. " You must be calm before you go, and you must be prepared to stay for some little time. My mother has sent me for you ; she begs you to come. If you are staying in the house, you can be of much more use than if we have to send for you. Will you help us ? Mrs. Chaloner will not object."

" I am sure that she will not. And if she does I cannot help it. I must come."

He waited while she made the few little preparations that were necessary. She took

his arm at the door, not that she needed
physical aid, but that contact with his strength
seemed to give her new resolution and support;
and, almost in silence, they went together to
the other house.

Mrs. Brendon met them in the hall. For
the first time in her life she took Lenore into
her arms and kissed her. Her face was white
and worn, her eyes dulled with watching, her
dress disordered. Cecil's danger had taken all
care or thought for herself out of her mind.
She was anxious for him, and for him only:
for his sake she even welcomed Lenore, whom
she had never professed to love.

The girl was taken with small delay to
Cecil's room. For the last three days he had
lain in a stupor, which had now been succeeded by violent delirium, and the doctors
were seriously alarmed about his state. No
trace of the person who had committed the
assault was to be found; the weapon, presum-
ably a heavy stick or bludgeon, had dis-

appeared; and it was not known that Cecil had any enemies who were likely to attack him by way of wreaking some wild revenge. At least, so it was said; but when Max heard these words, he could not but think of James Lloyd and the enigmatic expressions used by him with reference to Ruby Roslyn and Cecil. Was it possible that Lloyd had attacked and nearly murdered the man who had won Ruby's heart away from him? Surely it was not possible; some ruffianly tramp or thieving vagabond must have set upon Cecil and been frightened away before his robbery was achieved. This seemed the most plausible explanation; and yet Max was conscious of an uneasiness which he did not like to acknowledge to himself.

During the first hours that elapsed after Cecil was carried home by the men who found him upon the Quay, Max was too much occupied with many arrangements and anxieties to take steps towards the discovery of the truth.

In an emergency it seemed natural that the
whole household should lean upon him; even
Mrs. Brendon acknowledged that at such a
time he was invaluable; and it was not until
the following morning that Max could find
time to look after his own business, and to
learn from his father that the matter had been
put into the hands of the police, and that
the cowardly ruffian who had been guilty of
such brutal violence would, it was hoped,
speedily be discovered and lodged in gaol.

Max was snatching a hasty breakfast when
his father told him all this, and he made very
little comment.

"I cannot imagine what took Cecil to the
Quay at that hour of the evening," said Mr.
Brendon at the close of his communication.
"Can you ?"

Max shook his head. A suspicion of the
truth had flashed across his mind, but he did
not want to give utterance to it.

"I suppose," his father continued, more

slowly, that this could not have arisen out of that—that—Roslyn affair, could it?"

Max compelled himself to laugh, though his heart was heavy within him. "Cecil could have mastered Ted Roslyn, I think; and who else could there be?" he said.

But when he rose from the breakfast-table, where he and his father had taken their coffee alone together, Max determined to do something for himself in the way of detective work. No doubt it was of a simple and amateur kind, but there was a possibility of its succeeding where professional skill might fail.

He went straight to Dobell Terrace and asked for James Lloyd. He was at once admitted into a little back-parlour where Mrs. Lloyd was busy removing the breakfast things; she stopped short with a frightened air when she saw Max, but she did not seem disposed to be silent, and at once launched out into a flood of lamentations respecting "the accident to Mr. Cecil," of which she had just heard.

Max listened and said nothing for a time. Then he asked a question. "Is James very busy just now?" he said.

"Not very, sir; at least he's sometimes busy and sometimes not," was the rather confused answer. "And I'm glad that he should get work in London rather than here."

"In London! Is he gone?"

"Oh, yes, sir; he went by the four-forty train yesterday afternoon."

"Four-forty." Max stood and reflected. Cecil had been at home, alive and well, at four-forty. "Are you sure that he went by the four-forty?"

"Quite sure, Mr. Max. I don't know why you should doubt my word," said Mrs. Lloyd, with a touch of ready offence.

"I don't doubt it; not at all; I only wanted to be certain. Did you see him off at the station?"

"Yes, I did; and so did the children; and Mr. Bracy, too, if you like to inquire of him," said Mrs. Lloyd, still unappeased. "We all went down to the station together, and saw him off by the four-forty train; and sorry we were to do so, it coming so unexpected like."

"Unexpected, was it?"

"Yes, indeed, sir, on account of a letter that he got in the course of the afternoon. He packed a bag and said that he would send for his things later, and off he went, without so much as leaving an address. The least we could do was to see him off at the station, although he did not seem to want us very particularly."

There was nothing for Max to do after this but to take his leave; but he went straight to the railway station to make inquiries. There he learned that Lloyd, who was well known at the station, had indeed taken a ticket for Euston; that nobody had observed anything remarkable in his manner or appearance, and that his whole family and several friends had accompanied him to the station.

" That seems plain sailing enough," Max
said to himself as he turned away ; " and yet
it is quite possible that any one wishing to
conceal his movements might take a London
ticket, and leave the train at Beckley Junction,
tramping back over the fields so as to reach
the Quay between six and seven in the
evening. He could get away easily at the
junction. I 'll go over and inquire. Poor
Jim ! I never thought I should be tracking
him down in this way. But, after all, a
brother 's a brother, and one can't stand by to
see him half-killed without wishing to punish
the guilty man."

But inquiries at Beckley Junction proved
fruitless. It was a large and crowded place,
the meeting-point of many railway lines ; and
a young fellow like James Lloyd, of not very
striking appearance, would easily escape observation. Max was baffled, and returned home
regretting the time that he had wasted, and
hoping that after all Lloyd might be innocent

of the crime laid to his charge. He called
afterwards to get the young man's London
address, but could not obtain it. Mrs. Lloyd
declared that she still did not know it, and
although Max scarcely believed her, he was
obliged to come away unsatisfied. All that he
could do now was to wait until Cecil should be
able to answer questions. *He* might know who
his assailant had been, and set Max's mind at
rest upon the point; until he was conscious,
there was certainly nothing more to be done.
The fact that made Max most suspicious of
James Lloyd was this difficulty in getting his
London address, for he believed that Mrs.
Lloyd was purposely concealing it.

All this, however, occurred at the beginning of Cecil's illness; some days had since
elapsed, and there seemed no likelihood of
his returning just yet to health and strength.
In his delirium he called constantly for Lenore;
and the doctor had advised Mrs. Brendon to
send for the young lady whom he wished to

see. There was just a chance that he might
know her and be soothed by her presence. So
Lenore was brought to the Brendons', and
treated at once by everybody as a daughter of
the house.

It was a great shock to her to see Cecil in
his delirium, to hear him calling for her, and
yet to know that he did not recognise her face,
but she bore the ordeal bravely. She preserved
great calmness, and was careful to obey the
doctor's orders with exactitude. To sit by
Cecil's bedside, and take his hand in hers now
and then, to answer in soothing words when
he called for her, to lay cool cloths and ice
upon his burning head—these were all the
things that she could do for him ; but she was
ready and willing to spend her whole time and
strength upon the work. It seemed super-
fluous now to remember that she had been
angry with Cecil; she knew only that she
loved him, and that she would gladly give her
life for him if he required it.

He certainly became calmer and quieter from the moment when she entered the sick-room. There came a day at last when the fever had left him, and he could understand that she was at his side. He was weak as an infant; too weak to do more than look at her or whisper a word or two at a time; but it was plain that her presence gave him the deepest satisfaction. But at this point old Mrs. Chaloner interfered. She had not objected, she said, when Lenore was summoned to soothe Cecil in his delirium; the case was urgent, and not to be judged by ordinary rules; but now, surely *now*, the need for Lenore's presence had passed away, and she could be spared. Mr. Brendon tried to impress upon her the fact of Cecil's extreme weakness and the inexpediency of grieving or exciting him; but Mrs. Chaloner had been hurt by some injudicious comments of ill-natured acquaintances, and declared that, as Cecil was now conscious, Lenore must come home . at

once. And for one whole day Lenore was
kept close at her grandmother's side.

It was a hard day for Cecil and his nurses.
His weakness was very great, and seemed to
be increasing. His constitution was not
naturally strong, and the doctors were still
uncertain as to whether he would recover from
the effect of the attack made upon him.
Throughout the hours of that day his strength
seemed to fail more and more. It was then
that he managed to whisper a few words that
startled his father exceedingly. "Lenore ; I
want Lenore," he had murmured. "Let her
be my wife before I die." And with his son's
hollow, beseeching eyes fixed upon him, Mr.
Brendon had not found it in his heart [to
refuse an assent. He went, as usual in perplexity, to Max, and told him what had
occurred.

"Yes," Max answered, gravely. "I know he
wishes it. He said so to me last night. He
has set his heart on it."

"Mrs. Chaloner would never consent, you know."

"I think she would."

"And Lenore would refuse."

"No; you're wrong there," said Max, with a half-sad smile; "Lenore would consent. And then we should have the right to take care of her afterwards if——"

"It won't come to that; it won't come to that," said Mr. Brendon, moved out of his composure by Max's suggestion. "Poor lad! he's been weak, but never wilfully wicked, eh, Max? He'll get better and outlive us all, you'll see. But it's hard to refuse him anything just now."

"We must not refuse him," said Max, with some urgency. "Indeed, it would be a good thing, if the excitement is not too great for him. Lenore can manage him better than any of us. Look how he has lost ground to-day. We must have her back!"

They consulted the doctors; they spoke

once more to Cecil, whose heart was certainly
set upon his project. " I am dying," he said
to Max, to whom he spoke more freely than to
his father. " Let me show her that I love her;
that I have loved her all the time." And so,
at last, the matter was made conditional upon
Lenore's refusal or consent. Mr. Brendon
himself went to the Red House, and bore her
away almost by force to Cecil's bedside. It
was Cecil who should breathe his own request
into her ear; by this time they were sure that
she would refuse him nothing.

She needed no urging. " If you wish it.
Cecil," she said gently, " it shall be done."
Mrs. Chaloner's horror and distress had simply
to be disregarded. Lenore was of age; she
was able to act for herself. She and Max,
between them, made the necessary arrangements. A few hours had to elapse before it
was possible for the marriage-rite to be per-
formed, but until that time Lenore was
suffered to be almost entirely with Cecil. His

strength was gradually ebbing away; it sometimes seemed doubtful whether he would even
live to call Lenore his wife.

The day and the hour arrived at last, and
Lenore stood—a mournful bride—at his bedside. With pale lips and trembling hands
the two plighted their troth, promising to love
each other and be faithful one to another until
the end of life. The end did not seem far off
to them just then! To those who witnessed
it, the scene was a very touching one; it was
heart-rending to look upon these two, so soon,
perhaps, to be separated, plighting their troth
—"until death us do part," as Cecil faltered
out; fighting, as it seemed, all the time with
the enemy whose dread grasp was laid on his
heart and life. The rite was as short as possible; and for a little while they were left
alone together, hand in hand, looking at each
other with the long loving gaze, with which
for the present both seemed to be half content.
Lenore now and then rose to attend to the

doctor's orders, or whispered a few words of love, but nothing distracted the watchfulness of Cecil's melancholy regretful eyes. He made a sign at last that he wished to speak. She was obliged to place her ear close to his mouth to distinguish the words that he strove to say.

" You forgive me ? " she heard, and there was something more that she could not catch.

" Dearest, if I have anything to forgive, I forgive it; but I have nothing. Darling, don't look so distressed ; I can forgive anything, because I love you so dearly."

His eyes grew a little quieter, and his pale lips tried to smile. " My wife," he said, as if there were something inexpressibly soothing in the sound ; and then his eyelids quivered, fell, rose once more, half closed again, while a film gathered over the failing eyes ; and how terribly those catching, panting breaths, with long intervals between each, struck upon the ear of the listening new-made bride ! The doctor came in, stood by the bedside, and shook his head.

" It will soon be over," he said, in answer to Lenore's agonising imploring look. "A few hours, and then——"

She could not bear to hear any more; she turned back to catch her husband's last look; it might be that he would still murmur some dying word of love.

CHAPTER V.

But, after all, Cecil did not die. He struggled past the crisis into deadly weakness, and past the weakness into slow and painful convalescence. Little by little he gained strength and vigour; little by little he grew more able, day by day, to delight in the strange, new experience of Lenore's society, to hear her talk, to look at her as she moved about his room, even to make her laugh and blush at the pretty compliments he paid her. Never was there so satisfactory a marriage, everybody said. Mrs. Brendon was vexed about it certainly; she had missed the glory and excitement of a grand wedding and breakfast; but, on the other hand, nothing excites friend-

83

liness more than a bit of innocent romance,
and as soon as Cecil grew better Mrs. Brendon
declared herself "inundated" with notes and
cards and "kind inquiries" from all her
friends and relatives. Lenore had, of course,
taken up her permanent abode at the Brendons'
house; an uncomfortable state of affairs for
her, which, however, she willingly endured for
the sake of being with Cecil.

As for Cecil himself, he was very happy.
He may perhaps have been a little surprised at
finding himself so much in love with Lenore,
but the surprise was a pleasing one. It had
not occurred to him that there was anything
selfish in his resolve to marry her just as he
believed himself dying. On the contrary, he
thought it a matter for self-gratulation that he
had been so devoted as to wish to leave her
his name and a claim on his father's property.
Lenore took almost the same view of the
question. It was true that their hasty
marriage did proceed from pure love, but

some men would have hesitated before linking
a girl's name to theirs under such circumstances. Some silent criticism of Cecil's
demeanour occurred to Max. "However," he
reflected half remorsefully, "if he had died,
poor fellow, I believe it would have been a
consolation to Lenore to think of him as her
husband. Only, I don't fancy he sees that it
was in the least a *concession* on her part. But
neither does she; so they are quits." Miss
Roslyn seemed to have passed out of everybody's mind. Mr. Brendon secretly congratu-
lated himself on having rescued Cecil from her
clutches. Cecil thought of her occasionally,
but decided that Lenore should never be
distressed by hearing about that unlucky
stolen interview upon the pier. He had no
intention of confessing his errors to his wife.
It was an easier way to forget all that had
passed before his illness; to resolve to be a
better man for the future, and to bask in his
present felicity, than to begin married life with

a humiliating avowal of weakness which would lower him in his wife's eyes, and perhaps render her duties to himself less pleasurable. Cecil had strong notions of the honour due to a husband, but far less definite views respecting a husband's duties. Wifely duties appeared to him just now so very delightful, that he never thought of a time when Lenore's attendance on himself must necessarily be less exclusive, that jars would certainly occur in domestic life, and that if this ideal state of happiness were to continue, it must be founded upon absolute trust and mutual respect. There was just the lurking consciousness in his mind that he had behaved meanly to Ruby : the dread that in some way the details of his conduct should come to Lenore's knowledge ; the more stinging conviction that Lenore's distrust, if once aroused, would be hard to overcome. But these were mere pin-pricks of conscience. In general he was well protected from them by a sense of his

own good intentions, which had always been
to make people happy as long as they were in
his company; and he had great confidence in
the stability of Lenore's love for himself. For
as he maintained one evening when he was
getting well, and Lenore was making tea for
him and for Max, who had come up to see
them, "everybody knows that love will never
change."

"I don't know," said Lenore. "I think it
may."

"Then it was never a true love," said Cecil,
who always took a romantic side; "for if it
were it would survive every trial and every
danger."

"Question!" said Max, below his breath.

"Of course, I am speaking of women,"
observed his brother, with a slight increase of
colour. "Men are less constant, but a woman's
love ought to be 'strong as death.'"

"Strong as *life* would express something
more, perhaps," Lenore said, thoughtfully;

"it seems easy to think of death with a person one loves, but one needs almost more strength to live with and for him."

"You braved death with me," said Cecil, in a low tone, as he put his arm round her for a moment; "now try living with me instead. If you come out of one trial as well as of the other, darling, you will do splendidly."

There was another point on which Cecil maintained impenetrable reserve. He would give no hint, even to Max, as to the identity of the man who had attacked him on the pier. "What does it matter?" he said, in a half-lazy, half-languid way, which greatly irritated his father, although Mr. Brendon was taking a more indulgent view of Cecil's foibles than he had ever done before. "I could not see the fellow's face; perhaps he mistook me for somebody else. Perhaps he wanted to take my watch and chain. Who knows? You'll never find him now; it's nonsense to think of it."

" Have you actually *no* idea as to who it was ? " Max asked him abruptly when they were once alone together.

" If I had," said Cecil, lazily, " I should hold my tongue."

Max turned and looked at him for one moment, and went away satisfied in his own mind that Cecil was perfectly well aware of his assailant's name and motive.

James Lloyd had not returned to the town. Mrs. Lloyd still professed ignorance of his whereabouts, but Max did not believe her. There was a furtive, frightened look in her eyes which belied her words. However, there was nothing further to be done. If Cecil chose to be silent, Max acknowledged that the search must be useless. And by degrees the matter was dropped and half-forgotten by the world at large, although there was a strange, uneasy consciousness on Cecil's part, and a strong suspicion on that of Max, that it was Cecil's own weakness which had led a once

well-meaning, honest lad very nearly to incur
the guilt of murder.

Ruby Roslyn had left the town, and was
paying visits to her friends. She had scarcely
been seen abroad since Cecil's serious illness
was first known, and report did not credit her
with deep feeling about the matter. Max
heard more than once that she was looking
worn and ill, but that her spirits were unusually high, and that she was on the point of
an engagement to a young Hartpool manu-
facturer. Max shrugged his shoulders, but
was not ill-pleased by the news. He would
have been delighted to hear that Ruby was
well out of the place, once and for all. He
had a vague sense of danger—danger to Cecil,
danger perhaps to Lenore—in connection with
Ruby Roslyn. And he had a keen dislike to
her for the way in which her influence seemed
to have affected poor James Lloyd, who had
been as much the victim of her coquetry as of
Cecil's weakness.

Max had been too busy and too anxious to see much of the St. Aidans or of Miss Lingard of late, but as soon as Cecil was stronger, and began to talk of a sojourn in the Riviera by way of a honeymoon trip, he resumed his old habits of going to Gay Street two or three times a-week. He thought that Miss Lingard looked a little worn and tired, as if she had some cause for anxiety or pain. He wondered if she were well, and questioned Ursula in a vague, roundabout way concerning Miss Lingard's health and strength. Ursula had cultivated her friendship with Miss Lingard to an amazing extent: she spent a great deal of her time at the Priory, and was on intimate terms with all its inhabitants. She reported with some wonderment that Miss Lingard was perfectly well, and that she did not seem to have troubles or worries of any sort.

"Everybody has troubles and worries of some sort," said Max, drily.

"Have you?"

"Of course.   Business matters."

"I think," said Ursula, reflectively, "that that poor woman, Alice—the woman you picked up in the road, do you remember?—is the only worry that Miss Lingard has just now."

"How is she 'a worry'?"

"She is so fond of the children, you know, and Dolly is devoted to her; it is quite funny to see that child with her; and Miss Lingard says that she feels a little anxious sometimes, because—well, because Alice is not quite in her right mind, you know, and one does not know what she may do or say."

"Why does Miss Lingard keep her there?"

"I don't know: she seems fond of Alice and troubled about her too.   It sometimes seems to me as if she had known Alice before —or as if Alice were a dear friend or relation. Could that be so, Max?"

Max remembered Magdalen's strange words to him, the strange light in her eyes, on the night when he had helped to take Alice to the Priory. There was some mystery here which he could not understand. But he answered rather sharply:

"Don't be so fanciful, Ursula. Miss Lingard had never seen the woman before: she told me so. But she ought to send her away; it is hardly safe to let her stay there with those children."

"Tell her so."

"I could not take such a liberty. Besides, Miss Lingard is quite capable of managing her own affairs."

Max turned away with rather a vexed look in his face. Why, even while he acknowledged Magdalen's capacities, did he always wish so much to take upon himself the burden of her sorrows and her anxieties? He was ever conscious of a desire to help her; and yet she was a woman who gave rather than took help in her relations with others. Perhaps he was not free from the purely mascu-

line conviction that, however wise and good a
woman may be, she is never quite so wise and
good as the most ordinary specimen of man-
kind.

He had not time for much thought about
Magdalen, or for anything but his own affairs
just then. Cecil's absence threw a great deal
of labour and responsibility upon him, especially as Mr. Brendon's vigour seemed to be
failing a little. His chemical works were not
so remunerative as they ought to have been;
and he was made anxious from time to time
by complaints on the part of an agent for the
Malton property, which belonged to Captain
Esher. The fumes from his works were declared to be excessively injurious to the
Malton park and plantations, and he was
threatened with a lawsuit on the matter.
Expensive law proceedings, even if he were
to be successful in the long-run, would bear
hardly upon his resources; he was desirous of
avoiding them, although he had his father's

capital and experience to fall back upon, and
knew that they would never be wanting at a
pinch. He was hoping to compromise
matters with the Malton agent, and, while
still anxious, he did not foresee that the
cloud which had appeared in his horizon was
one which would by and bye cover the
whole heavens, and place him in utter darkness.

Cecil and Lenore went to Mentone. Mr.
Brendon took a house for them in Higher
Scarsfield, and furnished it with great care;
it was a pretty place, not far from the Priory,
known as " Chalgrove." For the present,
however, bride and bridegroom were not expected at their new home; Cecil's health was
far from strong, and it was thought advisable
for him to remain in an equable climate for
some months to come.

Into the midst of the busy and fairly pros-
perous life that Max had made for himself, a
sudden sorrow came with the force of a thun-
derbolt.

He went to his father's private room late one night, and found him busy over some papers.

"I have been putting these in order," he said, pointing to a pile before him on the table. "If anything should happen to me, you will know where to find them."

"Nothing is likely to happen to you at present, I should think," said Max, covering his anxiety by an assumption of the odd, blunt manner which his father understood so well.

"No, nothing that I know of. But death comes to all of us, sooner or later. Cecil will have to take another partner in when I am gone."

Max stood and waited for further indications of his father's state of mind.

"Of course the girls and your mother are well provided for," proceeded Mr. Brendon; "but there is one thing I should like to say to you, Max. Your mother is sometimes a little hasty, particularly with you and with Ursula; but I hope that as long as it is possible for you to hold on together you will. Cecil won't trouble himself much about his sisters; you must take my place to them;—do you hear?"

"Very well, father. But I don't see why you need trouble yourself now about so remote a contingency."

"It may not be so remote as you think. There's no knowing what may happen. I might never have another opportunity of saying these things to you. You are fond of Ursula, and she of you; don't abandon her, whatever you do. I have made you trustee and guardian, with your mother, to the two children, should I die before they are of age. You remember that I spoke about ·it before, and explained to Cecil why I did not care to burden him with the responsibility. He has a wife and may have children of his own by and bye. And you will be more thoughtful for the girls than Cecil would be, and I should like you to have a voice in the matter of their education."

"I should like to have a voice now," Max could not help saying. "Mother is making the girls work too hard."

"I must see about that. I will speak to her to-morrow. And I know you won't shirk this responsibility?"

"Certainly not, if I am ever called on to fulfil it."

"That's it; that's what I wanted to hear you say. I have always been able to trust you most fully, Max; you have not been like Cecil, who, with many good points, is never steady enough to gain one's confidence. I cannot depend on him. *You* have never given me half-an-hour's anxiety in your life."

Max felt repaid for a good deal of worry and much hard work when his father said these words.

"I will try to do my best for the future, as I have tried to do it in the past," he said, with a certain proud gratitude which his father fully appreciated. "But I don't like to hear you talk in that way, father; you know you're a young man yet, and will live to see your grandchildren about you for many a long year."

"I do not think that I shall see many years," replied Mr. Brendon, quietly; "though, as far as I know, I am well and strong enough at present. Well, I must finish my work; it is getting late. Go to bed, boy; it's time that young folks like you were asleep."

Max smiled at the notion of his requiring sleep at the untimely hour of twelve; but his father sent him off peremptorily.

"Good-night, my lad," he said, giving his hand to the young man; "good-night. God bless you. Don't wait for me; I shall soon have done. I am tired already."

Max left him, and thought little more on the subject. But the conversation recurred to his mind with startling distinctness a few days later, for Mr. Brendon was found one morning in the quiet sleep from which there is no awakening. He had died in the night from heart-disease.

CHAPTER VI.

A WALK IN THE RAIN.

IT was a wet, windy evening in April. For many hours had the rain been loading the laurel leaves and soaking the fragrant brown earth of the empty flower-beds before a certain house in Higher Scarsfield. This house, which stood well back from the road, was nearly opposite the Priory, and had been selected by Mr. Brendon for Cecil's residence upon his marriage. Thither, upon this chilly, stormy night, Cecil brought his young wife home.

Max and Ursula were there to receive them. Max was due at Gay Street about eight o'clock, and intended to take his sister home before that hour; but Cecil was so much horrified at the prospect of Ursula's wet walk

101

that Lenore insisted on keeping her for the
night. It wanted twenty minutes to eight
when Max started upon his walk back to
Scarsfield.

As the front-door closed upon him, and he
walked down the gravelled path, from which
the most distinct objects to be seen were the
tips of Miss Lingard's cedar trees, swaying
slightly, and defined in black layers against
the sky, Max's thoughts reverted with satisfaction to the scene of luxurious warmth,
brightness, and domestic happiness which he
had left indoors. It was a pleasure to know
that Cecil was comfortably settled and his
flirtation with Ruby Roslyn at an end. Max
deliberately preferred to believe that a man
with so loving a wife as Lenore would no
longer find a difficulty in being constant. He
was disposed to think well of Cecil; and it
did not occur to him, with his meagre
experience in love matters, that marriage does
not always fix a man's affections unalterably

upon the woman to whom he has given his hand. It did strike him that Cecil's buoyant spirits might have been sobered with advantage. Perhaps, considering the manner in which his marriage had actually taken place, and the events which had succeeded it, Lenore's future would have been safer had he felt a little less self-confidence in entering upon this new phase of his life. In outward bearing he had gained : his old sulky listlessness of manner had passed away, and improved health had partially robbed his face of its effeminate delicacy. Lenore, on the contrary, did not look the better for her year abroad. Her face was pale, and her eye anxious; but her mouth had won a steady sweetness which helped to give her an older appearance than she had possessed in her girlish days. Both of them had exclaimed at finding Max so little changed; though what change they expected to see in him was difficult to say. A close observer might have thought that his

face bore increased signs of care and responsibility in the deeper fold between his
eyebrows, and the added infrequency of his
slight, cool smile ; but Cecil and Lenore, not
being close observers, noted only that his
easy carelessness of attitude, and keen, quiet
glance, were the same as ever, and declared
him unaltered. Max half smiled at the
remembrance of their laughing verdict as he
turned away from their door into the wind
and rain.

He looked up at Miss Lingard's cedar trees,
and began to think of the rainy night when
he had helped to carry a helpless outcast
through those iron gates, and of another time
when he had been detained at her house by a
storm.

"Rain seems to be the first condition of my
meeting with her," he said to himself, casting
a long glance back to her house, and forward
down the hill. "It is wet and stormy enough
to meet her now."

And, indeed, he soon caught sight of a tall, dark figure in the gloom, which he thought must surely be hers. Half-a-dozen strides brought him up to it. Contrasted even with Ursula's bright beauty and Lenore's delicate loveliness, he could not help thinking that the pale grave face, turned towards him from a background of darkness, was the sweetest he had ever seen. Its very seriousness aroused in him a sense of sympathy, and a relieved consciousness that something which had been secretly jarring upon him was no longer present. The three whom he had just quitted were too sanguine, too untroubled for him. Here was some one who knew that life was not all play and pleasantness, who had a sort of religious tenderness for other people's souls and bodies—a tenderness of which he felt the subtle charm, but could not understand. There was an attraction about Magdalen which had led strangers even to confide their histories to her, which made her the special confidante of those who were in any kind of trouble. Max did not know that she possessed any peculiar power of winning confidence; he only knew that now and then he was irresistibly attracted into giving her his own.

"We are bound to the same place," she said to him, as they walked on together.

"Yes. I am going to take Mr. St. Aidan's class amalgamated with my own."

"It will be hard work, when both classes are so large."

"Perhaps so. But I like to have plenty to do."

"You are not in want of work generally, I suppose?"

"No," said Max, with an answering smile. "I think I may say I have had plenty to do since I left school at fifteen."

"You were young." Magdalen was aware that Max's life had differed greatly from that of Cecil, the elder son; and she was curious enough about it to ask the question,

" Did you leave school so early by your own wish ?"

" No ; by that of my father." Then, as if he saw some mute wonder in her face, or were meeting some implied blame of his father's conduct, he went on quickly,

" It happened by accident—almost. The original plan was that I should not enter the office till I had been to Cambridge. But the school broke up early one term on account of illness, and I came home and managed to make myself useful to my father. He soon thought that he could not easily spare me, and I—well, 1 was reconciled to the change sooner than you might imagine."

" The change must have disappointed you."

" You should remember what boys of fifteen are like, Miss Lingard. The sense of importance, freedom from school trammels, pride in my father's praise and in being of use to him—a good deal of self-conceit, in short—soon consoled me for the disappointment. For the time being I did feel it keenly, I acknowledge."

"Yes, indeed! When one loves study for its own sake, it must be terribly hard to be cut off from it."

"I don't know that I did love it for its own sake," said Max, bluntly. "The presumption is that I did not, or I should not have succumbed so easily."

"Whatever you felt then, you must have some love for it now, or you would not be so anxious to foster it in others."

"Oh, the working men?" said Max, with an air of receiving a new subject for consideration. "I don't know whether that is the real reason. I'm a working man myself, and I like to be among my fellows. I have been at business nearly all my life, you see; I've done nothing else since I was fifteen."

"Nothing?" she asked, with some significant emphasis.

"Nothing worth speaking of. And pro-

bably I should have done nothing more under
any circumstances. I was the dolt of the
family."

" Who said that ?—your masters ? "

" People in general," said Max ; then smiling at her half-suppressed exclamation of un-
belief, he added, " It was quite true. My
brain was hurt by a fall I had in my child-
hood, and I never learnt anything—not even
my letters—till I was ten years old. Surely
that fact shows how little I was fit for anything but what Mr. St. Aidan calls ' money-
grubbing.' "

" Mr. St. Aidan never meant to depreciate
any honest and manly work," said Magdalen,
warmly.

" No, no ; I am sure he did not. But
there was some truth in what he once said
—that money-making seemed with some men
more like an instinct than an exertion of
intelligence."

" I should think that your own work requires a fair amount of intelligence," observed his companion, noticing a certain perverseness in his manner of replying.

" It requires some forethought and some technical knowledge—that is all. And it has not even the merit of being pursued for un-selfish ends."

" For what end do you pursue it ? " Magdalen asked, point-blank.

He hesitated a little before answering, and spoke at last in a balanced, measuring sort of way, as if he wished to avoid a direct reply.

" I suppose I have various ends in view. There is the end of making good soap, which I have lately taken up. There is the hope of underselling one's neighbours, and of gaining a little credit for acuteness in the commercial world. There is the supreme object and aim of making money. Then there is the excitement of speculation in some kinds of business—such as that of my brother's—

and it is as keen an excitement as any to
be found at a gaming-table."

" And, in some respects, of the same
nature."

" Just so. Half of it is pure gambling."

" But this gambling is not an essential
part of business ? "

" I don't know whether we can avoid it.
One can scarcely avoid it and make money
as fast as I and most men would like to do."

" I can hardly wish you to make money
on those terms, Mr. Brendon. Must I say
that I cannot wish you success ? " said
Magdalen, with a smile which proved that
she scarcely thought him sincere. He
smiled too, but was in earnest as he answered :

" My wishes are more likely to prevail
than yours. As the world goes, I believe I
have a fair chance of success. Failure now
will come by my own fault or my own foolish-
ness."

" You are confident."

"I hope I am not over-confident. Mine is not the lot I should have chosen in life, but, such as it is, I mean to make the best of it."

" You would be a severe judge," said Magdalen, reflectively, " of people who had made great mistakes."

" No," he answered, rather hastily; " no, I hope not. At any rate, I would not judge wrong - doing harshly—sin, as people call it. I think one is justified in coming down heavily on folly."

" Yet folly is more excusable than sin in most people's eyes."

" I suppose so."

The reply was unsatisfactory to Magdalen's ears, and for a little time she kept silence.

The rain had stopped, and the high wind had partially dispersed the clouds, through which a fitful glimpse of the moon could now be seen. Looking to the right hand, Magdalen perceived, at the extremity of a wide street, a tall building, dimly lighted, that stood upon the river bank.

"Are not those your chemical works, Mr. Brendon? I have never been quite sure."

"They are, indeed. The wind is this way; don't you catch a whiff of the gases?"

"They are not very pleasant."

"Worse; they are very destructive. They, and the fumes from Bidness, have a good deal to answer for in the way of destroying vegetation. It is impossible to build chimneys high enough to carry the fumes away. I hear that the beauty of the Malton estate is quite ruined, and that the proprietor begins to talk about compensation. I expect that he will be in Scarsfield soon, demanding damages."

"The proprietor!" Magdalen's voice shook slightly.

"Brute that I am!" thought Max to himself, with a sudden remembrance of a report

which he had heard from his mother's lips,
but never quite believed. "Her voice sounds
as though she were frightened. Can it be?"
But aloud he said quite tranquilly, "Yes,
Captain Esher. He has not been here for
many years, I believe."

"He is the father of Dolly and Daisy," said
Magdalen, recovering her calmness by a great
effort of will, "and Mr. St. Aidan's cousin.
I hope he will not be hard on you, Mr. Brendon." She spoke lightly, but, as they passed
under a gas-lamp, Max saw that her face was
pale to the very lips.

Her composure was shaken, and not without
good reason. She had not heard anything of
Captain Esher for many months; the last
communication which she had received from
him was the letter respecting Alice Mackworth,
which had offended her so deeply. If he came
into the neighbourhood of Scarsfield, would
he not wish to see his own children? How
could she avoid him, if he visited Dolly and

Daisy at the Priory? And would he come to see, with his own eyes, the poor, half-crazed woman who was still under Magdalen's care, and whose first word had been Philip Esher's name? These were questions which had rushed into her mind with overwhelming force, and made that evening's work difficult to Magdalen.

She was hardly surprised on reaching home to find a note from Mrs. St. Aidan, couched in rather mysterious terms. " I want you to come to the Rectory as early as possible to-morrow. I have a matter of the greatest importance to talk over with you," wrote the Rector's wife. Magdalen smiled and sighed a little as she folded up the letter. She foresaw trouble and perplexity, for she had long been aware that Emilia St. Aidan had secretly espoused "poor Philip's cause," and thought that he was hardly treated for a mis-demeanour of his youth.

Magdalen presented herself at the Rectory

before ten o'clock next morning, and was at once taken up to Mrs. St. Aidan's boudoir, where that lady had been breakfasting. The Rector was away from home for a few days, so there was nobody to interrupt the conversation. Magdalen saw at the first glance that Mrs. St. Aidan was in a state of suppressed excitement. Her eyes and cheeks were brighter than usual; her pretty white fingers were a little tremulous. But Magdalen was resolved to take no notice of these signs; to ask no questions, and to show no curiosity.

"Magdalen," she said, after a few trivial and rather absently-spoken observations, "I have some news for you."

"For me, dear?" Magdalen had taken up a piece of embroidery on which Mrs. St. Aidan had been engaged, and was busily putting in stitches. .

"Yes, for you. It may affect your plans, perhaps. Philip Esher is coming back to Malton."

"So I have heard," said Magdalen, composedly.

"You have heard! From whom? It is not generally known."

"Mr. Max Brendon told me. He was interested in the fact, because Captain Esher wants compensation for damage done to the trees at Malton by the fumes from Mr. Brendon's chemical works."

"Magdalen! You take it very coolly!"

"How else should I take it?" said Magdalen, lifting her eyes for the first time to Mrs. St. Aidan's face. "What is Captain Esher's return to me?"

Mrs. St. Aidan bit her lip. "He is the children's father, at all events."

"You mean," said Magdalen, gently, "that he will want to see them. Is that likely?"

"Yes; he has written to me to say so."

Magdalen put down her work. Her eyes wandered reflectively about the room for a minute or two. Then she answered with

perfect serenity; "Of course he must see
them, then."

"And you too."

"That is scarcely necessary."

"My dear!" exclaimed Mrs. St. Aidan,
with much emphasis, "do you know what
you are saying? If he comes to your house
to see them, he is sure to see you too."

"I do not think so. I shall give orders
accordingly. He will never be shown into
my presence."

"And you know so little of Philip Esher as
to think that he will not find his way to you
when once he is in your house?"

Magdalen's face flushed. "You speak," she
said, slowly, "as if you had some knowledge
of his intentions. *I* should never have
supposed for a moment that he would try
to see me; *you* seem to think that he will.
What reasons have you?"

"A letter from him."

"I thought so. Will you let me see it?"

"I would rather not, dear. It is meant for my eye alone," said Mrs. St. Aidan, with some embarrassment. "But I may tell you this much : he means to see his children, and he means to see you."

Magdalen's lip quivered. She leaned back in her chair and reflected for a few minutes. Then, she said, almost passionately :

"He can only strike me through the children. If they were not with me, he would have no pretext for coming to the house."

"That is what Gervas and I have always said. If you really wanted to keep him away, you should not have taken charge of his children."

Mrs. St. Aidan stole a glance at Magdalen to see how she took this speech, but Magdalen did not seem to hear.

"Emilia," she said, more abruptly, than was usual with her—"Emilia, help me out of the difficulty. Let the children come to you for a few weeks' visit. Then he can have no pretence for coming to the Priory."

"My dear child, I would if I could!" sighed Mrs. St. Aidan, "but it's impossible. Gervas says that he cannot accept the responsibility. I did ask him, but he thinks that it would be only shirking the difficulty, and that you would have to face it sooner or later."

"That is quite true," said Magdalen, in a dejected tone. "Quite true. But I do not see—*why*—Captain Esher should want to visit me."

"Then I'll enlighten you," said Mrs. St. Aidan, with more of her wonted briskness. "He wants to visit you because he intends to ask you to become his wife."

CHAPTER VII.

PEACE OR WAR?

MAGDALEN rose to her feet; a burning red came to her brow; her eyes flashed. The excitement lasted only for a moment, however; she sat down again, her face paling as she spoke.

"He will not dare," she said.

"Not dare! Is there anything Philip will not dare if he has set his heart on it?"

"Emilia," said Magdalen, desperately, "I have never told you all. It is my firm conviction that his wife is not dead. I am almost assured in my own mind that the poor woman who was carried into my house some months ago is Alice Mackworth."

"Magdalen are you mad?" Mrs. St. Aidan

sat up very erect, with the flush deepening
upon her face. "If she were alive, do you not
suppose that Philip would own her?"

"I am not sure."

"At any rate, he would never speak of
marrying again."

"Can we be sure of that?"

Mrs. St. Aidan spoke almost angrily.
"What a man will do when he is young and
foolish is nothing to go by now. Besides,
I never quite understood that story, Madge.
I believe that Philip *thought* that his wife
was dead. Of course it was very sad—very
dreadful—very unfortunate for—for everybody, but I cannot think that poor Philip was
quite so much to blame as was said."

Magdalen kept silence. Her lip curled a
little, but she would not trust herself to speak.

"Tell me the grounds for your belief," said
Mrs. St. Aidan after a painful pause. "You
would not say a thing of that kind without a
reason."

Very quietly Magdalen related the circumstances of Alice's arrival at the Priory. Mrs. St. Aidan had never heard the whole story before. She was not convinced by it.

" You have ridiculously little to go upon," she said. " I wonder that you condemn a man on such slight grounds, Magdalen. He denied it, you say ? "

" Yes."

" Did you tell Gervas ? "

" I did."

" And he did not believe it ? "

" No. And for that reason he did not wish me to tell you, but I think that you ought to know."

There was another silence. Magdalen sat looking at her hands, which were clasped before her in her lap. On Mrs. St. Aidan's mobile face various expressions testified to the rapid workings of her mind. At last she stretched out her hand and touched Magdalen's.

"Forgive me, dear, if I have spoken hastily," she said. "I know your feelings —I know how much you were wronged. But I was brought up with Philip; he was like a brother to me for many years; and I cannot bear to think him wholly bad. Oh, Magdalen, it is such a grief to me!"

The tears fell from her eyes as she spoke. Magdalen, softened at once by the sight of her friend's agitation, bent forward and kissed her on the forehead.

"Dear Emilia!" she said. She could add nothing more. It was impossible for her to think of Philip Esher as Emilia desired, and she felt that it was better to be silent. Mrs. St. Aidan wiped her tears away, and then took up an embroidered silk bag which lay on the couch beside her. From this bag she took a letter.

"This was enclosed in one to me," she said, handing it to Magdalen. "Don't be

angry with me, dear. He entreated me to
give it to you, and I cannot bear to refuse him."

Magdalen held the letter in her hand
for a moment, with a blank look upon
her face. The envelope bore no address.
" Is it for me ? " she asked.

" Yes, dearest. Read it, Madge ; for my
sake, if not for his."

Very slowly, and very reluctantly, Magdalen opened the letter and read.

This was what Philip Esher wrote :

" MY DEAR MISS LINGARD,—My last letter
received no answer from you. Perhaps it
did not deserve one. I have scarcely the
courage to write again ; and yet, something
in my heart tells me that you may not
have forgotten me altogether; that I am
not too presumptuous in hoping that one
day you will forgive the past so far as to
let me call myself your friend. At any
rate, I trust that you will not forbid me

to visit my children, whom you have cared
for so devotedly. Perhaps when I see you
I may induce you to believe a little in my
regret for the past, and my ambitions for
the future.—Yours, with sincere regard,

"PHILIP ESHER."

"It is a clever letter," said Magdalen,
coldly, as she laid it down. "But he asks
too much." She crushed it together in her
hand as if in a sudden spasm of pain. "He
is presumptuous."

Then she straightened out the crushed
letter, and gave it to Mrs. St. Aidan, who
read it with eager interest.

"Do you call that presumptuous, Madge?"
she asked, rather wistfully. "Considering
Philip's disposition, I should scarcely have
thought it possible for him to write so
humbly. What shall you do?"

"Oh, he can come to see his children, if
he pleases," said Magdalen, in her gravest
and coldest tones. "Would you be so kind

as to tell him so when you write,
Emilia ? "

"And you will see him yourself ? "

The old colour, the old light, flashed into
Magdalen's face and eyes. "Never—if I
can help it," she replied.

Mrs. St. Aidan paused, and then said
softly,

"Magdalen, dear, excuse me if I say that
your refusal looks as if you were afraid of him."

Magdalen's lips curved in a slight dis-
dainful smile ; she did not seem to think
it worth while to answer. Mrs. St. Aidan
began to feel irritated by her serenity.

"You are hard on him," she went on.
"What can a man do but express his
sorrow for past wrong-doing ? Is he never
to be forgiven ? I thought your creed was
that no sin was beyond forgiveness, no sinner
too bad to be reclaimed ? Do you make
Philip the one exception, because he injured
you ? "

"Oh, Emilia, it is you who are hard now," said Magdalen, gently. "I certainly think that all sin can be forgiven to a repentant sinner—forgiven by God."

"You remind me of that story about Queen Elizabeth," said Mrs. St. Aidan, sarcastically. "What was it she said to the woman who had injured her? 'God may forgive you, but I never can.' That is your attitude, Magdalen, towards Philip Esher; I leave it to you to decide whether it is a Christian one."

"You are mistaken," said Magdalen, with energy. "You misunderstand me completely. I do not think that I have any personal grudge against Captain Esher. But it seems to me that I have no right to treat him as though he had never erred. It is the *consequence* of his wrong-doing, not the *punishment*, Emilia, that I feel his presence an offence to me. I cannot help it. God knows that it was not always so; I loved

Philip Esher once; but I have reason now to thank God that I have been saved from the misery of linking my fate to that of a shameless and godless man."

Magdalen's face was pale; her eyes were on fire. Not for years had she been so much moved; perhaps she had never spoken so freely before. Mrs. St. Aidan murmured some soothing, imploring words, but they did not avail to silence her; she felt that she must now say what she had to say, once and for all.

"If," she said, "Philip Esher insists upon meeting me, I must meet him, but not as a friend. He must be changed indeed before I could forget the wrong that he did to those children's mother, to the children themselves. We have no right—you and I, Emilia—to look on him as an honourable, high-minded man, whom we can trust. I may be forced to let the children see him, but I will not be forced into friendship with him."

"My dear, nobody wants to force you—

unless it be Philip himself; but do think of
the children."

" Of the children ? "

" Philip has a perfect right to take them
away from you if he chooses; if you offend
him he may do it. Would it be good for
them to be brought up in his way, amongst
his friends ? "

Mrs. St. Aidan showed a good deal of tact
in making this suggestion. It struck Magdalen powerfully; the colour came and went
in her face, and her mouth trembled.

" No," she said. " No, indeed."

" Then be prudent, dear. I do not ask you
to show him more than civility. But let him
come to the Priory and see the children.
Very likely he will not care to come more than
once or twice."

" I have said that he may come to see them."

" But see him yourself, Madge. Don't avoid
him ; don't show, if you can help it, that you
are afraid of him."

The eyes of the two women met, and Magdalen's fell first. A rush of burning colour to cheek and brow almost startled Mrs. St. Aidan, who was not used to seeing Magdalen blush so painfully. There was a momentary pause, and then Magdalen rose to her feet.

"I must go," she said, in an altered voice. "I ought to be at home. I have a great deal to do. Good-bye, Emilia."

Mrs. St. Aidan drew her face down and kissed it, but she did not venture to allude again to the message for Philip. She felt that she had said enough, although she had not said all that she meant to say. For Philip Esher was already in Scarsfield, and Magdalen had not been told.

She was not long to be kept in ignorance. Captain Esher presented himself at the Priory that very afternoon.

Magdalen was sitting alone in the bare and business-like little room in which she transacted most of her affairs. She was writing

letters, and had given orders that she was not
to be disturbed.   It was with some surprise
therefore, that she heard a low knock at the
door; but supposing it to be from one of the
children, she called out "Come in," without
raising her head from the hand on which it
rested.   She was weary and languid after her
exciting discussion with Mrs. St. Aidan, and
she did not look up until an unfamiliar step
and movement attracted her attention.

"Who is there?" she said, suddenly.

" I hope I do not interrupt," said Captain
Esher, politely, but in as common-place a tone
as if he had been in the habit of seeing her
once a week.

Magdalen rose, without haste, but with the
greatest dignity, and confronted him.   Her
eyes gleamed and her face was paler than
usual, but she showed no trace of embarrassment in her manner.   She bowed slightly,
as if to a stranger, and quietly asked a
question.

"May I inquire what your business is with me ? "

It was like a declaration of war. Captain Esher looked at her steadily, and allowed himself a little smile. He thought that he understood her very well—as he understood all women. But he had a good deal to learn about Magdalen.

Before he had been two minutes in the room, he had subjected every detail of furniture and of Magdalen's dress to subtle criticism. He was simply amused by the ascetic plainness of the room, the absence of ornament from her dress. Her face dismayed him somewhat; it was so calm, so grave, so different from the girlish face that he used to know, that he absolutely began to consider whether it were worth while to overcome the aversion that she felt, or pretended to feel, for him. But it piqued his vanity to think that a woman should so easily forget an old love, and that his presence should have so little power

over her. This, at least, was not to be borne
he would make her speak to him as an old
acquaintance, at any rate. And he would
begin the attack at once.

Magdalen was thinking meanwhile how
little he was changed. The slight figure, not
very tall; the cropped golden brown hair and
heavy moustache; the broad, well-developed
forehead, straight eyebrows, and long, brilliant
dark eyes—a rare combination of colouring,
which was repeated in Dolly's child-face—
these were unchanged still. The only dif-
ferences she could find lay in the lower part
of his face. A slightly unequal curving of the
nostrils, a habitual curl of the lips, had been
deepened by time into a perpetual sneer.
There was more fulness of outline about
the chin than in old times, more pressure
about the mouth; and these changes, small as
they were, gave to the whole face an expression of scorn and cruelty, not lessened by
the piercing coldness of his fine eyes. It was

a face of some power and much refinement; but, more noticeably than ever, the face of a man who had all his life been bent on his own pleasure, and who never forgot or forgave a wrong.

He now permitted himself to assume a look of confusion and distress. " I thought," he said, apologetically, " that you had consented to see me. Otherwise, I could not have dared to intrude. Mrs. St. Aidan told me that I might come—to visit my children."

" To visit your children—yes," said Magdalen. She turned to ring the bell. " I will send for them at once. My servant made some mistake in showing you into this room ; I trust that you will excuse it."

Her voice was calm and untroubled, but cold as ice : her eyes met his without flinching, as she stood erect near the mantelpiece, waiting for the servant for whom she had rung. Captain Esher looked at her with admiration. He had not known that

Magdalen could be so stately, so magnificent.

He made a step forward, as if moved by an impulse that he could not resist. "Magdalen," he said, slightly opening his arms as though to clasp her to his breast; "Magdalen—I did not come to see them : I came to see *you!*"

There was no sign of emotion on Magdalen's face. She looked as if she had not heard a single word. And at this moment the maid appeared in answer to her summons : Magdalen noticed that she looked guilty and frightened, as if she knew that she had done wrong.

"Show this gentleman into the drawing-room, Jane, and then find Miss Dolly and Miss Daisy and send them here to me."

The maid waited for the visitor to follow, but Captain Esher, bending his brows and pulling at his long moustache, did not move from the spot. Magdalen looked at him : he made her a courtly bow.

" I follow you," he said, in a low tone. " I can wait until you are ready."

Magdalen made a gesture of anger—a rare manifestation in her.

" Find the children, Jane," she said, over her shoulder, to the maid : " I will show the way to the drawing-room. Captain Esher—"

As the door closed, he interrupted her.

" I told you," he said, "that I came to see you as well as the children. Are you not going to listen to me ? "

" You can have nothing to say to me."

" You mean that you have nothing to say to *me*. And do you think that I am going to leave my children in the care of a woman who will not even speak to me ? "

The words were softly spoken, but there was a threat within them for all their softness. Magdalen had turned towards the door, but as she listened her hands fell to her side, her foot halted. After a moment's pause, she turned to him again.

"What do you want?" she asked, in a different tone.

A gleam of triumph showed itself in Captain Esher's eyes. He had touched the right string now: in time, he thought, he should get all that he desired.

"You have given me leave to see my children; I thank you for it. But I want sometimes to see you too. I want to meet you as a friend."

"We are not friends: we never can be," she answered, coldly.

"How is it possible," he murmured, "that I should leave my children in the hands of one who is not my friend? Do you think that I wish my two little girls to grow up to hate me?"

"As far as I have anything to do with your children," she said, resolutely, "I shall teach them to honour their parents."

"Is it possible," he asked again, "that my enemy can teach them to honour—*me?*"

" I was never your enemy. I am not your enemy now."

" Then be my friend, Magdalen," he cried, stretching out his hands towards her ; " forgive me the wrong that I once did you, and be my friend."

Magdalen drew herself away from him without a word of answer. Her look, her movements, were enough : Esher saw what she meant. He uttered a bitter exclamation.

" So this is what your Christian charity comes to ! You cannot forgive an injury, it seems: you cannot forget that I once erred— although it was from love of you. You have decided the point at issue, Miss Lingard, in your own way : I suppose you are prepared to take the consequences."

" What consequences ? "

" I will take the children back with me to Malton. They cannot stay here unless you will treat me with civility. I reassert my claim. My children shall come with me."

"Oh, no, no, no!" cried Magdalen, suddenly turning white and clasping her hands before her. "You would not take them away! Anything—anything but that!"

As she spoke, and Captain Esher stood regarding her with a cruel smile upon his handsome face, the door softly opened, and two fair childish heads appeared. "You sent for us, Maidie," said little Daisy's soft voice. "Shall we come in?"

CHAPTER VIII.

WAR.

THE entrance of the children effected an immediate diversion. Magdalen turned to them with relief. She had meant to prepare them in private for the meeting with their father, but as this was now impossible she made the best of the matter, and told them quietly their visitor's name. It was rather a curious meeting. Captain Esher had not seen his little daughters since the day of the interrupted wedding at Riversmead, when they were only three years old. In spite of his expressions of anxiety and affection concerning them, he did not scan them with a very loving eye. He cared little for children in the abstract, and for these two in particular, he was con-

scious of something approaching dislike. He
knew, however, that it would be unwise to
show his true feeling, and resigned himself to
play the part of the affectionate father. With
Dolly, bright, vivacious, saucy, and singularly
like himself in appearance, he soon divined
that he could easily get on ; Daisy, shy,
sensitive, and silent, irritated him from the
first moment by her evident fear of him. It
was, perhaps, against Daisy, too, that she so
strongly resembled her poor mother.

Further private conversation was impossible,
and Magdalen was only too glad to escape
from Philip Esher's company, and to regain
her calmness by quiet thought in her own
room. The children were bidden to enter-
tain their father for a little while, and they
acquitted themselves well. Even Captain
Esher was astonished and pleased with their
intelligence, their good manners, their pretty,
dainty, little ways. Dolly soon forgot all
shyness with him, and as she was a child of

whom any man might well be proud—brilli-
antly beautiful, clever, original, and vivacious
—he speedily succumbed to her fascinations,
and developed a liking for her at which he
was half-surprised and half-amused.

The children led him into the drawing-
room. He knew the place well, and looked
about him with interest as he entered it. In
the days when he had been old Miss Esher's
favourite and reputed heir, he had planned a
thorough transformation of this old room.
Its slightly faded splendours had not satisfied
him. Now he was pleased to see that Magdalen had changed nothing; the old silk
hangings, the Chippendale chairs, the gilded
mirrors, were exactly as they used to be in
Miss Esher's time. A rush of anger came
over him when he remembered the way in
which he had been, as he phrased it, "de-
frauded" of the old place. Magdalen had
no business to possess it; it was his by right,
and his children's after him. He vowed to

himself that he would get it back again at
any sacrifice. The house—and its mistress
—should be his one day.

He smiled as he remembered the bareness
of the room in which he had found her. He
did not believe that she had not expected him
to come that afternoon. Her reception of
him had been a bit of finished acting, he
thought; the *mise-en-scène* was perfect, and
Magdalen was a consummate coquette. Well,
she should be punished for her coquetry,
sooner or later, and the children should be the
instruments of her punishment.

It was nearly four o'clock when the children
were called to see their father. In half-an-
hour's time, Dolly came running to Magdalen, her face glowing with delight.

"He is such a nice papa, Maidie!" she
exclaimed. "I love him so much, and he has
promised us all sorts of things; a lovely fan
and a pearl necklace for me from Paris, and a
doll for Daisy, and we have asked him to stay

to tea. He sent me to ask if you would let him."

"Of course, if he likes to stay, Dolly. You can have tea in the drawing-room. I will tell Miss Jessop about it. Now run back to your papa."

"Miss Jessop!" said Dolly with a twist of her shoulders; "why should you tell *her*? Papa won't want *her*, I'm sure."

Magdalen hushed her.

"Your papa does not know how kind and good Miss Jessop is, but you do, so I do not like you to speak in that manner, Dolly. Miss Jessop will come to pour out tea. Your little fingers can't do it."

"But why won't you come?"

"I am going to have tea with Alice and old Mrs. Milner upstairs."

"But why? Just when papa is here too!"

"Run away now, Dolly; that will do," said Magdalen, with the accent of gentle dignity that imposed obedience even upon

Dolly's wild spirits. The child ran back to the drawing-room without another word, and Magdalen went to find Miss Jessop and request her to give Captain Esher his cup of tea.

"But, my dear Madge," said the old lady, with many a flutter and stammer, "are you sure—do you think that it's right—I was never so much surprised in my life as to see Captain Esher here!"

"Do not let us speak or think of the past," said Magdalen, quietly. "I cannot keep his children from him. There is no necessity for me to see him again."

No one would have guessed from her tranquil manner that she felt as if her heart were burning itself out in a passion of indignation at Philip Esher's presumption, an agony of jealous fear for the children whom she could not protect from the father that she distrusted. She went about her usual affairs in her usual way; presiding,

as she often did, at the table, where two
or three humble pensioners took their afternoon meal, wondering all the time, with her
ears strained to catch every sound from the
drawing-room, when her unwelcome visitor
meant to go. When tea was over, she
hesitated for a few moments as to whether
the usual routine of her household should
go on, or whether she would alter her cus-
tom while Captain Esher was in the house.
She was in the habit of conducting evening
prayers immediately after tea—a practice
which ensured the presence of the children
and her more infirm visitors. She usually
had some half-invalid strangers in the
house—pale needle-women from London, in
want of country air, an ailing homeless
governess, perhaps, or a sickly child whose
parents could not afford to send it away
from home, and for their good she had
adopted various little rules and customs
which she knew would be greatly at vari-

ance with Philip Esher's ideas. She put down her hesitation to cowardice, and was ashamed of it; she resolved to go on as usual, without taking any notice of his presence in the house, but at the same time she was conscious of a thrill of proud reluctance at letting him know how greatly she was changed. She felt sure that this reluctance was sin, and mentally castigated herself for it, but she could not get rid of it altogether.

Meanwhile, Captain Esher had had his tea with the children and Miss Jessop. The old lady disappeared immediately afterwards, and at a quarter to six a bell began to ring. Daisy was standing rather timidly by her father's chair, while Dolly sat on his knee, when Captain Esher glanced at his watch, and asked what the bell was ringing for.

"It's time for prayers," said Daisy, glancing at her sister.

"Prayers! What prayers?" asked Captain Esher, in an amused tone.

"We have prayers every evening in the great hall, papa."

"Prayers in the hall! Good heavens! Read by the old lady, I suppose, to the servants?"

"No; Maidie reads them. I think we ought to go, Dolly."

"Magdalen!" murmured the Captain below his breath, as he caressed his moustache to hide a slow smile. "What a transformation! Yet I don't know——— And are *you* obliged to attend Divine worship in the hall?" he asked aloud, in a tone of which the ridicule was not lost upon Dolly's quick ears.

"Yes, papa," said Daisy. "We have a hymn, and Maidie reads; it is very nice to have it so early, or else the old people and the children would have to go to bed without hearing it."

"And I wish we did," muttered Dolly, who had been in a perverse mood all day. "I don't see the good!"

"Oh, Dolly, how can you be so naughty?" said Daisy, with grave eyes.

"Little Methodist!" said her father, half-aloud. "Never mind, Dolly; you are papa's own daughter in your dislike of cant."

Dolly understood only that papa was rather pleased that she did not care for prayers, and cast a triumphant look at Daisy, who had moved towards the door.

"May I go, papa? Maidie likes us to come."

"Take me with you," said her father. "I should like to hear it too, for once." And, though Dolly pouted and hung back, Captain Esher was accordingly escorted by his little daughters to the hall.

When the little assembly had dispersed, Captain Esher approached sufficiently near to say in Magdalen's ear—

" What sort of a play is this ? Tragedy, comedy, melodrama ? A new version of *I Puritani?* "

" I am not acting ; I am in earnest," said Magdalen.

" Miss Lingard as *la belle Puritaine* is a novelty to me, you must remember."

She stopped short in her slow walk towards the door, and seemed, by the fire in her eye, to be about to reply with some vehemence ; but she met Daisy's wondering glance, and turned back with lips more compressed than usual. The children followed her ; their father came behind.

" Must you go now, papa ? " said Dolly, possessing herself of his hand as they reached the hall.

" In a few minutes. First of all, I want to speak five words to Miss Lingard, if she will grant me audience."

Again Magdalen looked at him, this time with merely a grave, considerate expression, a little weary, as though she wondered when this trying visit would be over. He understood the look well enough, but he had yet a bold stroke to make, which Magdalen had unconsciously suggested to him.

She led the way into her sitting-room, and stood upon the rug by the window with her face turned towards the garden outside. Not once, as he noticed, had she seated herself in his presence.

Captain Esher half-extended his hands, as if he would instinctively have taken hers, yet knew that she would not allow him to do so; an effective gesture of entreaty, well seconded by the softness of his eyes and voice.

"Magdalen—forgive me for using the name," he said; "forgive me too that I for a moment doubted your sincerity."

"My sincerity? I can scarcely see why you should doubt it."

"Not now—not since I have seen you and heard you pray like the saint you are; no,

I am not mocking, Magdalen; and, believe
me, it is no small tribute from *me* to acknowledge your sincerity.".

"Is it?"

"I see; you do not believe in mine. You
are very just; inplacably just, Magdalen; but
your own Scriptures tell you to 'love mercy'
in the midst of justice, do they not? I ap-
pealed to old memories, to your recognition of
the fact that I was those children's father,
before; now I will appeal to your own goodness, for I feel that you are a good woman."

"What do you want?" asked Magdalen,
abruptly. "I do not wish to be flattered,
Captain Esher, and I do not know what you
can require from me, now that I place no
obstacles in the way of your seeing the children when you please."

"I ask only for what you can give easily,"
said Esher, with a look of humility; "help to
make me a better man than I have been. My
life has been wild; I have erred in many ways,

and my heart wearies of sin and error, Magdalen. I come to you; I see your exquisite faith, •your sweet devotion; I envy you the beliefs that once I shared—that now I long to share. Teach me, as you have taught my children, to believe."

He came nearer as he spoke, but Magdalen did not answer; she was looking into the gathering dusk, and he could not see her face. Was she touched or not?

"I do not ask now for your friendship, and it would be profanation to dream of love," he went on, in low distinct tones; "but let me be to you as the heathen, Magdalen, whom you would gladly instruct; I have little more knowledge than they. Let me be your scholar —I shall be a docile one—and teach me the simple truths that I have forgotten."

"Forgotten? yes; but you learned them once," said Magdalen, so sadly that he fancied, with a sudden thrill of hope, that his request would soon be granted. "In old days you did not profess to know so little of the truth."

"I tried to make myself better for your sake—then. And since I lost—forfeited—the hope of you, I have gone from bad to worse; I own it freely. Now I would gladly change. Help me, Magdalen."

"I am not the right person to help you; it is of no use to come to me."

"You are the only person who can help me in this world."

"Not so," said she, with tremulous decision. "There are God's authorised ministers——"

"What! Magdalen, do you think I should go to a priest?"

"There are churches open; there is God's Word that you can read."

He turned away with a scornful laugh. "It is not these that I want. They will do me no good. I want *your* help, Magdalen."

"I will give you my prayers," she said, mournfully; "I can do nothing more." Her voice took a softer, sweeter inflection as she added, "I have prayed for you all these years, Philip; it would be my greatest comfort, my greatest blessing, to know that I have not prayed in vain."

Philip's heart gave a bound of triumph. His silver tongue had carried him far indeed! She had called him by his first name; she had acknowledged that she prayed for him. What more might he not expect?

"I thank you," he said, in a low, moved voice. "I thank you from the bottom of my heart. I know that I can ask for nothing more. Your goodness has touched me very deeply. Will you forgive me my foolish words this afternoon about taking the children from you? Not for worlds would I remove them from your influence. Let me see them some-times—let me see you; it is all I ask. Your friendship is too high a boon."

"It is not that," said Magdalen. Her

voice had grown tremulous, and she sank into the seat that he proffered her, as if her limbs were weak. "But surely you forget all—all —that passed between us. We are the last people—the last people in the world—who can be friends."

"Then let us be something more," he said. It was a daring stroke, and one which he repented as soon as it was made. The room was nearly dark, and he could not see Magdalen's face. The silence that fell between them was so deep, so pregnant, that he scarcely dared to breathe. But it lasted only for a moment. She rose from her chair and spoke in the voice of icy coldness which he was learning to know so well.

"I think there is no more to be said. Pray come to see your children as often as you please, Captain Esher. I am too busy to receive visitors, but the little girls will be at liberty whenever you like."

"Is that all?" he said in low, muffled tones.

"You will make no truce with me, then? You refuse to help me, Magdalen?"

"I can do nothing for you, Captain Esher."

"Then I am thrown back on my own resources," he said in a voice that was gentle — indeed, almost tender — though his eyes glanced with an expression of bitter anger which made her start. He went on deliberately. "You will not wonder if I cause my children to infringe your rules sometimes? Of course I shall have nothing to guide me; I shall not know how you wish them to be brought up. Suppose I unwittingly say to them things of which you do not approve? You know that I have very little belief in what you teach them. Whose influence will be the greater in the long run, I wonder, yours or mine?"

"What do you mean?"

He laughed. "It would be *piquant* to hear my sceptical notions from Dolly's baby lips, would it not? If you will not help me to correct my wrong ideas, you must not grumble if I convey them to her mind. I fancy that she will prove an apt scholar."

A great fear came into Magdalen's eyes. She pressed her hands tightly together and spoke with a new vehemence. "It is useless to leave me their bodies if you mean to steal away their souls," she exclaimed, half involuntarily.

"My dear Miss Lingard," said Captain Esher, politely, "you need have no cause for alarm. Give me the inestimable boon of your friendship, and I promise you that not a word shall pass my lips to which priest or governess could object. I acknowledge that I don't answer for my prudence otherwise."

The sneer, the veiled threat, offended Magdalen. She turned from him with grave disdain, refusing in her own mind to believe that he would try to influence the children against her teaching. He saw that he would gain nothing more from her that night, and so,

with a low bow and a few words of courteous
farewell, he took his leave. The children
were waiting in the hall to say good-night;
Magdalen heard his cool, amused laugh and
their ringing, merry voices through the half-
open door, as she sank with a faint, exhausted
sensation into the nearest chair. There was
relief in knowing at last that he had left
the house. Relief — was there also some
regret?

"I was a fool to think for a moment that
she had gone off," said Philip Esher to himself,
as he walked slowly to the Rectory, where
Mrs. St. Aidan was anxiously awaiting him :
"she has gained in expression and manner;
she moves like a duchess, and her eyes are
magnificent. When her fanaticism brought
the colour to her cheeks and fire to her eyes,
she was twice as handsome as she used to be.
Ah, my lady, I'll make you ask my pardon
some day for the insults you have heaped on
me, to-night!"

CHAPTER IX.

CAPTAIN ESHER'S TACTICS.

It occurred to Captain Esher on his way to his hotel to wonder a little that Magdalen had not named Alice to him—the homeless vagrant whom she had, as he thought, so unwarrantably connected with his life. He supposed that she had found out her mistake, or that the woman had left the Priory. This, however, was not the case. Magdalen was resolved that Alice and Captain Esher should one day meet; but on this occasion she had been taken by surprise, and had had no time to bring the two face to face. Besides, Alice was unusually weak and ill: she was almost entirely confined to her room by chronic bronchitis, and Magdalen feared the effect

upon her of sudden excitement.   For, whether
Alice were Captain Esher's wife or not (and
Magdalen now thought that she *could* not
be his wife), she had at any rate once been
deeply interested in him, and could still be
thrown into an alarming state of agitation at
the mention of his name.

Captain Esher had been asked to dine at
the Rectory, rather against the Rector's will.
But Mrs. St. Aidan insisted on his coming :
her affection for Philip Esher was not to be set
aside.   So the Rector had consented to receive
him once again.

Philip was a little late, but he made his
excuses very gracefully to Mrs. St. Aidan,
explaining that he had been visiting his
children, and that time had slipped away
alarmingly fast in their delightful society—
"delightful to a father, at any rate ; " and
that he had then had to go back to his hotel
to dress for dinner.

"Your paternal feelings have been in

abeyance rather long," said Mrs. St. Aidan. She could defend him behind his back, but she could not always govern her sarcastic tongue in his presence.

Esher shrugged his shoulders. "There were other circumstances to keep me away," he said, blandly, as though Mrs. St. Aidan were a stranger to whom that fact needed explanation.

"What do you think of the children, Philip?" asked the Rector, by way of diversion. "Beautiful little creatures, are they not?"

"Very. Dorothy is, I think, the prettier of the two."

"Dolly resembles you," said Mrs. St. Aidan, with a smile.

"Ah! I did not notice the resemblance," said Captain Esher, with a slightly conscious air of personal beauty, rather to be deprecated than otherwise. "Her hair is like mine, perhaps: as it used to be. They have been very carefully trained in Miss Lingard's peculiar views I should imagine."

The announcement of dinner fortunately cut short the conversation, for Mrs. St. Aidan's bright eyes were beginning to show that she was indignant. She refused to be wheeled into the dining-room, so her husband and Philip had the dinner-table to themselves, over which they talked politics and news of the day. The two men did not amalgamate well : they never had done so, and, when they talked of politics or religion, they were further apart than ever. Mr. St. Aidan was a Conservative and a High Churchman ; Philip Esher's opinions were too slippery to be easily seized and classified, but they ranged about in a haze of polite Agnosticism, and general disbelief in God or man. He had varied intellectual and artistic tastes, however, if he had no strong convictions of anything ; he had plenty of brain power although he seldom chose to use it, and he could talk so well on most subjects that his uncle was sometimes half-amazed to feel how little they had in common, and how few topics he cared to discuss with him. The sneering careless tone that it was natural to Esher to adopt about everything was one that the Rector particularly disliked. And when he disliked a man's tone, he was rather apt to retire into a shell of silence and look courteously fatigued, instead of arguing the points that he feared would be attacked. Captain Esher, too, never exerted his conversational powers without occasion, therefore dinner became a somewhat tame affair, and a return to the drawing-room was decided on as soon as possible.

They had just rejoined Mrs. St. Aidan, when a servant summoned the Rector into the hall, where stood a messenger from Chalgrove; he presently returned to explain that he was obliged to go out for a short time, but would be back as soon as possible, and after a few words in a low tone to his wife, he left her with his nephew.

"Parish business, I suppose?" said Captain Esher, with an ironical emphasis on the first word.

"One of our neighbours—Mr. Brendon—has sent for Gervas to baptize his little girl, a child only a very few hours old, and not expected to live."

"Brendon? I know that name, I think. Max Brendon, owner of some chemical works? I did not know he was married."

"No; this is his elder brother, Cecil; son of old Mr. Brendon, whom perhaps you remember."

"Ah, yes. They were hardly in your set, I think?"

"We have known them much better lately —Max Brendon more particularly."

Esher looked up quickly. "You know him personally? Really, I am a little surprised."

"What have you to say against him, pray, Philip?"

"Nothing at all, my dear Emilia, save from a business point of view. His chemical gases have spoiled all my trees. I am rather sorry you know him well, for Stoner, my agent, calls him 'that impracticable young man.'"

"And why should it affect our knowing him?"

"For no reason. It may be a little inconvenient that I should have a lawsuit with him; but I dare say we shall arrange it amicably."

"I hope so."

"How did you make his acquaintance?—if I may ask the question," said Philip, lazily ensconcing himself in the depths of a comfortable easy-chair. "Your husband used to have rather an objection to business-men."

"Max Brendon is not at all an ordinary man," answered Mrs. St. Aidan, decidedly.

"He can both think and feel ; and his family is by no means despicable—his mother was a Grenvil."

"You remind me of the ancient epitaph, Emilia ; 'Sincerely pious, *and* first cousin of the Earl of Cork,'" said Captain Esher, maliciously.

"I never spoke of Max Brendon as 'sincerely pious,' did I ? I should be very far from the truth if I did."

"I thought he was your pattern young man."

"Gervas sees a great deal of him at a night-school that is held three or four times a-week." Mrs. St. Aidan ignored the last remark.

"Can't Mr. Max Brendon read and write ?" inquired Captain Esher in a sleepy tone.

"Philip ! what are you talking about ? Mr. Brendon goes to Gay Street to teach others, not to learn, of course. You are too absurd."

Philip suddenly grew wakeful, and changed his position to a sitting one.

"The night-school in Gay Street! The same place to which Magdalen goes so often, I presume?"

"Yes; Magdalen teaches there. How did you know anything about it?"

"Dolly told me," said Philip, lying back negligently. Then, with a slight, disagreeable smile: "Is this young man after Magdalen?"

"I confess that I don't quite know what you mean."

"I beg pardon. Does Mr. Brendon wish to marry Miss Lingard?"

"No one ever thought of such a thing," said Mrs. St. Aidan, looking so much startled that he was assured of her sincerity. "It would be most unsuitable; besides——"

"Magdalen has somebody else in her eye, I suppose?"

"I think it is time you dropped that name, and said 'Miss Lingard,' Philip."

"A slightly needless assumption of formality, don't you think?"

"Not needless, under the circumstances."

"So you are my enemy too, Emilia? I almost thought that *you* would have helped me."

"My help would do you no good. She will never marry you now."

"You think not," said Captain Esher, stroking his moustache. "I am not sure."

"You have certainly no mean opinion of yourself, if you think she will."

"I never found that it answered, to have a mean opinion of one's-self."

"I am surprised that you admire her still."

"She has grown into a very beautiful woman. You look amazed; but I think her far handsomer than she was in the days of her bloom. I admire her very much. She would make a fine tragic actress."

"So you saw her?" said Mrs. St. Aidan,

laying down her work and looking at him eagerly.

"Saw her? Excuse me, but for what other purpose did I go?"

"To see your children, you said."

"Ah, yes; I did say so, I remember. To see my children, of course. She said she would not admit me, I suppose."

"Are you going again?"

Captain Esher laughed, a low musical laugh that irritated Mrs. St. Aidan. "You are very curious, Emilia. Yes, I am going again— and as often as I choose. How long will you give me to conquer her in?"

"You'll never conquer her, Philip; so do not think of it."

"Six weeks," said Captain Esher, softly; and then he laughed again and went to the piano, where he began to play with exquisite taste and skill.

Mr. St. Aidan returned about ten o'clock and reported that the baby was a little

better, and that Mrs. Cecil Brendon was
going on well.   He had named the child
Cecilia, according to the mother's wish, and
Max Brendon, Ursula, and Mrs. Chaloner
were to be its sponsors.   Mr. St. Aidan
was much touched by the anxiety that
Cecil had displayed about his wife and
little daughter; "he was evidently quite
unnerved, scarcely master of himself," the
Rector said.   "I liked him very much,
though he is certainly different from his
brother, who is a diamond in the rough,
Emilia."

"Emilia has not lost her habit of finding out wonderful virtues in the most
unlikely subjects," said Philip Esher, smiling, as he rose to take his leave.   "I wish
her joy of her rough diamonds; I prefer
them polished."

Magdalen, meanwhile, had heard from the
children a most enthusiastic account of their
father.   Their hearts had been completely

gained by his amused, half-simulated interest in their sayings and doings. Dolly,
particularly, seemed to have been greatly
flattered and more caressed than Daisy.
Her tongue went at twice the pace of her
sister's, and Magdalen wondered, but could
not quite discover, whether the quieter
child had felt herself slighted for talkative
Dolly. Both children had some odd questions to ask, which it puzzled Magdalen to
answer prudently. " Maidie, why did papa
call me a ' little Methodist ' ? " " Were you
sorry that papa came, Maidie ? Why
wouldn't you come to tea ? He was very
vexed when you didn't come." " Why
aren't you and papa friends now, Maidie ?
He says you used to be, but you don't
like him now." At which Dolly burst out,
angrily, " I don't mean to love anybody
who isn't friends with my dear papa."
Magdalen found it expedient to hush the
conversation, which went on while she was

brushing their hair before they went to bed,
and to remind them that they usually
learned a verse or two before kneeling
down to say their prayers. But here again
she met from opposition from Dolly. " I
don't believe papa cares for our saying
prayers. I don't want to say mine to-
night."

The habit of obedience, and Magdalen's
grave surprise, brought the child back to
her usual submissive frame of mind. But
it was no wonder that Magdalen went
downstairs and spent the evening in a state
of alarmed dismay at the kind of influence
which Philip Esher evidently chose to exert
over his children.

Captain Esher stayed in Scarsfield, and
visited his children with laudable regularity
almost every day. But he seldom saw
Magdalen. She managed to avoid him,
although he laid several snares to entrap
her into an interview; he always came un-

expectedly, and once or twice met her in
the street; but she either eluded him altogether, or had a companion in whose presence
he could not speak.

This intercourse with their father produced
a notable change in the children. They were
in a constant state of excited expectation, for
he never came without gifts of toys, sweet
things to eat, ornaments or flowers, in his
hands. Magdalen expected him soon to tire
of the little girls' companionship; but his
patience seemed to be unwearied. Shut up in
her own bare little chamber, busy with needle-
work, for she suffered from a feverish
excitement of the nerves which would not let
her read or think connectedly, she heard
bursts of gay laughter, snatches of song,
merry voices, from the morning-room in which
they generally sat. Sometimes they crossed
the lawn, or went out for a walk, clinging to
his hands; and then, if he passed Magdalen's
window, he would look in, not rudely or

boldly, but with a sort of intentness of expression which showed that he was anxious for a glimpse of her. If he did not come for a whole day, Dolly grew restless and fretful; when he had been and gone, she became languid, as if the excitement had been too much for her, or else passionate and defiant, as though he had taught her not to brook contradiction. Daisy behaved more equably, but at times Magdalen could not account for a puzzled, saddened look on her little face, and was grieved at the alternations of feeling towards herself which both children showed, being now affectionate, now sullen or constrained. Miss Jessop, too, came to her with stories of Dolly's utterances and quotations "from papa," which Dolly had not dared to parade in Magdalen's presence, and which had made the good old lady's hair stand on end; irreverent expressions and doubts of all kinds about sacred things that Captain Esher had not scrupled to pour into her ears, being much diverted by the precocious avidity with which she imbibed anything that could justify her recoil from constituted authority. At first Magdalen said, "Patience : I will not impress those notions deeper on her mind by argument, unless I am obliged to do so. Her father will soon go away, I hope ; and she cannot forget all that she has been taught through a few careless words from him. She has said nothing of the kind in my presence, and I am not forced to notice what has been only accidentally overheard."

But the battle came at last. One Sunday afternoon Magdalen sat talking with Daisy over some Bible pictures, while Dolly lay on the sofa in a lazy attitude rather unusual with her. Magdalen had been explaining a picture and telling a Bible story in simple words, wondering meanwhile why Daisy looked so puzzled, when Dolly suddenly interrupted her by remarking—

"Papa doesn't believe all that. Papa says

that half the things you teach us are nonsense."

Magdalen laid down her book.

"What things, Dolly?"

"About the Bible," said Dolly, promptly.
"He doesn't believe that the Bible is true,
and I don't either."

"You don't believe that God's Word is
true? Dolly, my poor child!"

"I won't be called 'poor child!'" said Dolly,
sitting up with flashing eyes and crimsoning
cheek. "I am not poor, and I believe what
papa says; not what you do. Papa knows
best."

"Oh, Dolly, Dolly," said Magdalen, sadly,
"can this be you? My darling, listen to
me——"

But before she could continue Daisy had
burst out crying, and hidden her face on
Magdalen's lap.

"It is true, is it?" she sobbed. "You're
not mistaken, are you, Maidie? Oh, do, do

tell me! There is Somebody to take care of us up in heaven, isn't there? It's not a mistake?"

"No, my darling, it is not a mistake," said Magdalen, and then she added some simple, loving words about her own faith which had the effect of calming the sobbing child, and of making Dolly look half-sullen, half-ashamed.

Then Daisy turned to her sister with a flash of unusual indignation.

"Papa is wrong," she said, "and he is wrong when he says that Maidie does not really love us. She does—she does!"

Dolly uttered an inarticulate sound of dissent, and Magdalen, whose heart was bleeding within her, said gently but firmly—

"You must know that your father is quite mistaken. You know that I love you better than any one in the world."

Daisy put her arms round Magdalen's neck.

"Papa *shan't* be mistaken!" cried Dolly, bursting into passionate tears. "Daisy, you

don't love him, and Magdalen doesn't; but
I do, I do!"

The uncontrollable passion of the child was
most painful to witness, and Magdalen would
gladly have soothed her, but she struggled and
fought at the slightest touch, and would listen
to nothing. In the midst of it all came Captain
Esher's well-known ring at the front-door bell.

"It's papa; don't go away!" whispered
Daisy, anxiously, as his footsteps crossed the
hall.

"I am not going," answered Magdalen,
and sat motionless, her arm clasping Daisy
closer still.

Captain Esher took in the situation with
one keen glance. For some time he had been
expecting some such scene as this. Perhaps
he had not desired it to be a stormy one.
Magdalen rose and faced him, still keeping
her arm round Daisy; Philip bowed politely,
but his eye sought out Dolly, weeping tem-
pestuously on the floor.

"Dolly!" he said, in a quick voice, "What is the matter?"

In a moment Dolly was in his arms, sobbing out incoherent statements.

"I love you, papa, and they don't—they say you are wrong. I don't love Magdalen any longer; let me come with you. . . . She is angry with me——"

Magdalen saw Captain Esher bend his head and whisper something quick and short into his little daughter's ear. Dolly replied, aloud:

"No, she didn't punish me . . . but she talks and looks and . . . I want to be like you, papa, and with you always . . ."

"Has your system answered, Miss Lingard?" asked Philip Esher, over the child's head.

And Magdalen returned another question:

"How dare you say what you have said?"

"Whose fault has it been?" he asked, with a smile upon his face. "I warned you beforehand—quiet, Dolly; don't cry—and you must take the consequences."

"Must I see *them* deprived of their faith in my teaching?" said Magdalen, indicating the children by a slight movement of her head.

"By no means," and Captain Esher drew a long tress of Dolly's golden hair through his hand; "but you must see them follow their father's lead sometimes, if you put yourself in opposition to me. Dolly and myself against you and Daisy there, who clings to you so devotedly—who'll win? Do you throw up the game?"

"Let me send the children away, and speak without metaphors."

"Daisy can go if you like," he said, indolently, "Dolly stays with me."

"Then stay, Daisy," said Magdalen, sitting down wearily, as though her powers were leaving her. "Stay, and let me hear in *your* presence what your father wants."

The children held their breath, half-terrified; Philip looked at her with a cool, musing smile.

"I will make a bargain with you," he said, drawing nearer to her, and speaking in so low a tone that the little ones could not hear.

"Well?"

"I will say nothing that you can disapprove, so long as you stay in the same room with us whenever I come."

"Stay—with you and the children?"

"Yes, I will even contradict what I have told them."

"And—suppose I say 'No'?"

"On your own head be it!" said Esher, with an evil, mischievous look. "You have seen what I can do."

"Anything but *that*. For the present, then, I must stay."

"Thanks, although you do not give your consent with flattering readiness. Dolly," he said, softening his voice as he looked down at the bright head that leaned against his breast, "have you left off crying? What have you been troubling Miss Lingard about? You little fool, I never meant you to take what I said seriously. Believe all she tells you, and more too, if you like."

"You said—what she told us—was not true," gasped Dolly, with open eyes and mouth.

"I was teasing you then."

"And the Bible *is* true, and everything ?"

"Don't go into details, little one. Don't you hear me say that you are to believe all she tells you ?"

Dolly looked from one to another in grievous uncertainty. She had never thought that her father would deceive her, or amuse himself at her expense, and her disappointment in him was sudden and bitter. For the time being she returned to her old allegiance ; ran to Magdalen, and hid her face on her shoulder.

Captain Esher did not go away. He made himself comfortable in an arm-chair, talked unconcernedly to Magdalen, petted both his children. They had tea together, much to Miss Jessop's surprise, who could not understand her Madge's pale face and fixed grave eyes, though she saw well enough that trouble and anxiety were there. They all walked to church together, too, and then it was that Magdalen said abruptly, in a moment when the children were out of earshot :

"I am doing what you asked, after all ; but it is for their sakes."

"Don't trouble yourself to explain, my dear Magdalen ; I quite understand on what terms we are at present."

"I may not always be able to sit with the children when you come. You will not insist on my doing that ?"

"There can never be a moment when your presence is not most welcome."

"You will not talk about those things when I am away ?" she said, with a tone of painful entreaty in her voice.

"Well, perhaps not; so long as we are friends, Magdalen."

She sighed heavily, but did not now dispute the name.

CHAPTER X.

A STATE OF SIEGE.

A curious quietness came over the household after that stormy Sunday at the Priory. Dolly and Daisy, delighted at the pact made between Magdalen and their father, were nearly their old obedient, docile selves; and Magdalen seemed able no longer to contend with the influences that surrounded her. Captain Esher constituted himself her everpresent visitor and devoted attendant. He had found out her weak side, her vulnerable point—this passionate love of the children—and, by attacking it steadily and skilfully, he hoped to win her altogether for himself. He felt almost certain that she would not now quarrel with him while the children

187

were in her care, because she was afraid
that he would take them from her; and
he sedulously abstained from giving her any
definite assurance that they should remain
at the Priory. In fact, he purposely
dropped suggestions now and then that they
should be sent abroad or to school; and
enjoyed the expression of pain that came
to Magdalen's face at the mention of such
schemes, for he wanted to make her feel
his power.

Dolly soon found out that Maidie would
not refuse, if possible, what papa requested;
and she tried hard to gain indulgence by
working on his feelings with representations
of her hard fate in the schoolroom, where
she had to learn lessons with Daisy. Captain Esher had some moderation left; he
neither wanted to destroy Magdalen's influence, nor to have his children constantly by
his side; and accordingly, he was as thoughtful as one could expect a man to be about

not disturbing the routine of lessons, or taking Dolly out for a drive when Magdalen thought she was better at home. Daisy he left in the background. It was Dolly's enthusiastic devotion to himself, as well as her beauty, that had touched his heart; Daisy was too unobtrusive, too soft and quiet, to gain his affection. She clung still to Magdalen, who was thankful to keep the love of one, if not of both, of the children. Certainly Dolly's little heart seemed to have gone from her completely.

Magdalen made one effort to dislodge Captain Esher from his position, but failed to stir him an inch. She brought him face to face one day in the garden with the woman who called herself Alice Mackworth.

It was a warm spring day; so mild and balmy that the invalid had been brought out in a bath-chair to taste the sweetness of the blossoming year. She was sitting with her wan face turned to the west, whence

a flood of golden light was pouring as the
sun neared the horizon. Her long, thin
hands were crossed upon her lap; her blue
eyes rested languidly upon some brightly-
tinted flowers that Dolly had brought her.
Dolly had a strange liking for this silent,
half-mad creature, who had come no one
knew whither on that stormy July night;
and the poor woman herself was attracted
and interested by the golden-haired child as
she was by nobody else. Dolly could always
bring a faint smile to those bloodless lips;
she could even coax Alice to speak and to
eat, when every means of persuasion had
been tried and failed. Watching them together, Magdalen had often wondered whether
it was the tie of kinship that united them;
whether some subtle yearning sprang up between the woman and the child, yearning
of which neither knew the meaning, but
which unconsciously worked upon the heart
and mind of each. In a minor degree,

Daisy was also attracted by poor Alice; but with her it was merely a child's natural feeling of pity and tenderness for one who was sick and suffering. The odd and special fascination which Dolly seemed to find in Magdalen's guest was peculiar to herself alone.

Magdalen led Captain Esher to the place where Alice was sitting, without any preparatory word. She wanted to see whether he would recognise her or not, and whether she would show any sign of agitation in his presence. If it was likely to be a cruel experiment, she said to herself sternly that she could not help it. She was in peculiar circumstances, and was not to be bound by conventional rules. She thought that she should know the truth when she had brought Philip and this woman face to face. She led him up to Alice's chair, and then she looked at him.

"Do you know her?" she asked—so quietly that even Philip could not have guessed that her heart was beating wildly, and that her voice was almost choked by the fast-coming breath. "Do you know her?"—It was all that she could say.

Perhaps Philip was not entirely unprepared for some such scene as this. Dolly's chatter had already made him well acquainted with Alice's position in the house. He had been wondering when Magdalen meant to confront him with her; he knew that she would do it sooner or later. "Madge was always given to stage-effects," he said to himself, with careless contempt. "Fortunately, I am not a stage-villain to be scared into remorse by a chance likeness, or the trick of a stranger's voice and manners. She has mistaken her man."

He did not flinch then as he glanced at Alice's face. He raised his eyebrows a little and smiled—that was all.

"Is this your protégée?" he asked, in his usual negligent, easy voice. "Poor soul! she looks very ill."

Magdalen turned from him abruptly, to glance at Alice. The haggard blue eyes were lifted blankly to Captain Esher's face: there was no trace of recognition in their dull stare. Magdalen leaned forward and touched her on the arm.

"Do you know this gentleman?" she asked.

No answer: only silence and that vacant, unmeaning gaze.

"This is Captain Esher—Philip Esher," said Magdalen distinctly. "You said that you wanted to see him."

The woman shook her head.

"No," she murmured, as if speaking in a dream, "not I; it was not I. Take him away."

"Do you not know him?" Magdalen asked again.

There was no answer. She had turned her head aside like a tired child, and was playing with the flowers in her lap.

"It is no use distressing her," said Captain

Esher, softly. "Don't you see that her mind is completely gone?"

Magdalen moved away from the sick woman's side, with a gesture expressive of deep disappointment and chagrin.

"I hoped," she said after a moment's pause, "that the doubt would be cleared up at last— that now I should know the truth."

"I can tell you the truth," said Captain Esher, who was watching her with a stealthy look in his long, dark eyes, and a curious twitching of the muscles of the face. "If you would believe me, I could set all your doubts to rest."

Magdalen looked up quickly.

"Do you know her?"

"I do. It is Louisa Mackworth, my dead wife's sister."

"Can that be? She is not old enough for the woman that I remember."

"You do remember her? You saw her for a few minutes only."

"I know." Magdalen did not add with her lips what her heart said at that moment: "But I could never forget the face of the woman who brought me so much misery."

"She was seven years older than Alice," Captain Esher proceeded, slowly; "and Alice was only seventeen when I married her. She would be twenty-eight now—it is eleven years ago. Louisa Mackworth would be thirty-five. That woman looks thirty-five and more."

"Her life has aged her," said Magdalen, abruptly.

Captain Esher paused, and then resumed, with his eyes on the ground:

"Louisa Mackworth," he said, "had a scar on her left arm: the mark of a burn. Perhaps you know whether that mark is there now."

Magdalen's face flushed and then grew pale.

"Yes," she said, "there is such a mark on her arm."

"I have here," he continued, taking a small case from his pocket, "a miniature of Alice, and a lock of her hair. Take them and compare them for yourself with the woman before you."

Magdalen held out her hand. She opened the square morocco case, and saw a small painting of a woman's head, done on ivory. Below it was the word "Alice," in seed pearls. A lock of golden hair was coiled under the glass on the other side.

The face was that of a very lovely girl, fair, blue-eyed, golden-haired. It was not that of the woman whom Magdalen had called Alice for so long. The hair was of a different shade : it was brighter, more definite in hue. Even allowing for age and the lapse of time, with their dimming effects, it was hardly possible to suppose that that golden tress had ever been cut from the head of Magdalen's guest.

She closed the case and gave it back to its owner without a word. He stood watching her curiously.

" Are you convinced ? " he said at last.

" I suppose I must be," she answered, in a very low tone.

" You speak as if you were sorry."

He could not understand why a sudden flood of crimson covered her pale face, nor why she turned from him so abruptly and began to pace the garden-walk. He strolled by her side, thinking to himself that of all women Magdalen was the most incomprehensible.

He did not know that she felt as if a safeguard had been removed. As long as she could believe that Philip Esher's wife was still alive, there was no danger of his asking her to marry him, or of her being tempted to consent. Now that, against her will, she was driven to the conviction that his wife was dead, and that this woman was only Louisa Mackworth after all, she knew that she stood in a perilous position. Something in Philip Esher's eyes had already told her what he wanted; and she—she was not at liberty to repulse him, to treat him with merited disdain, because of the children who were so dear to her. She was in a cruel strait, and the way out of it was dark to her indeed.

It was with a slight smile upon his face that Philip spoke at last.

"You are very ready to believe evil of me, Magdalen," he said, "and therefore I offer you unlimited proof. I can give you the names of twenty of Louisa Mackworth's friends and neighbours in Manchester. They would identify her without hesitation: to me she seems wonderfully little changed. I will send for some of them, or you can send for them yourself, if you please. You might then feel satisfied that I speak the truth."

"It is needless: I am satisfied," said Magdalen.

"I trust that you will see that you have, for once, done me some injustice."

"Yes," she said listlessly, with her eyes on the ground, " I have, as you say, done you an injustice. I am sorry for it."

His eyes flashed. " Magdalen," he said, in his softest tones, " be sorry for me, too."

He had called her back to life at last ! She darted a superb glance upon him, drew up her stately head, and turned away from him to the children, who were playing on the lawn. For the moment he had offended her, and yet he did not think that he had gone too far. He was not ill-satisfied with this abrupt ending to their conversation.

It was not long before Mrs. St. Aidan heard of the newly-established truce between Magdalen and Philip Esher, and thought herself justified in coming over to the Priory to question Magdalen about it.

" You have set me wondering with the rest of the world, Madge."

" Why ? " Magdalen asked quietly, though with a troubled face.

"The world says that you are going to marry Philip."

"The world is wrong."

"But will it always be wrong? Oh, Magdalen, my dear, don't be hard. You might forgive him *now*."

"There are some things that a woman has no right to forgive," said Magdalen, rising up suddenly, as if to put an end to the conversation. "What I do, Emilia, is for the children's sake, not for their father's."

"Marry him for the children's sake," said Mrs. St. Aidan, intrepidly, "and then you will have them all to yourself. Philip would never be bothered with them then. But," she went on, with a rapid change of tone, "of course I did not come to talk to you about him, dear." Magdalen smiled a little bitterly. "I came to ask you to dinner on Thursday next. Do come."

"Who is to be there?"

Mrs. St. Aidan ran over a list of guests.

Philip was not among them; and Magdalen promised to come.

On Thursday evening, therefore, a very pleasant party of guests assembled at the Rectory. The clerical element was rather largely represented; but for this Magdalen was not sorry. She was a little surprised to meet Max Brendon; Mrs. St. Aidan had not mentioned him, in fact he had been asked at the last moment to supply the place of somebody else. Mrs. St. Aidan was very keenly watchful of Magdalen's demeanour, especially when she was taken in to dinner by Max Brendon, whom Captain Esher's words had taught her to look upon from a marriageable point of view. But nothing could be more un-lover-like than Max's manner, although it was evident that he liked Miss Lingard's company. And Magdalen *en grande tenue* always looked well; the style of dress that she adopted, although old for her years, suited her to perfection.

She wore black velvet, trimmed with old point lace; diamonds in her hair and on her neck. In spite of herself Mrs. St. Aidan wished that Captain Esher could see her in the full magnificence of her large and noble beauty.

And thus Captain Esher did see her. He had not been invited to dinner, and nobody could tell whether he had heard of the party or not, but in some mysterious manner he was found in the middle of the evening standing by Mrs. St. Aidan's sofa, lightly explaining that he had been obliged by business to see Mr. St. Aidan, who had brought him into the drawing-room. The hostess expressed her displeasure by a very frigid assumption of dignity, and glanced apprehensively both at Magdalen and Max; but Philip Esher took no apparent notice of her coldness, stayed beside her some moments, and only sauntered away when the piano was opened, and the Rector was asking

Magdalen to sing. Then he ensconced himself in a corner, with folded arms, and the
indifference of a man who is going to be
bored. In reality he was watching, with
eager eyes, every movement of Magdalen's
face and hands. She had never looked to
him so handsome as when she sat down at
the piano, the transparent paleness of her
face slightly disturbed by a faint carnation
flush, her large dark eyes less calm than
usual, her white bosom rising and falling
beneath the delicate lace and rich velvet
that covered it so softly. Captain Esher
was confident of success; it was clear to
him *she knew he was there*—that in itself
was a triumph, for she had never looked
his way, and yet her calmness had de-
parted. What would she sing? anything
that they both remembered? anything that
they had sung together?

He was disappointed. She sung a stately
old *canzone* which he had never heard

before. As she played the concluding chord she knew that he was standing at her side; his whisper fell hotly on her ear.

"Sing 'Tender and True,' Magdalen; that is the song for you," he murmured.

She rose and moved a little to one side. Some one asked Captain Esher to sing; it was well known that he had a very fine tenor voice. He smiled as he sat down at the piano, and glanced at Magdalen, who had not been able to move away altogether. "I will sing—*to you*," he said, in a voice meant only for her ear. But the words were a little louder than he had intended them to be, and were overheard by one listener at least. And this listener was Max Brendon.

Captain Esher dashed at once into a passionate love-song, which he had often sung to Magdalen in days gone by. It seemed to make no impression upon her. At its close he saw that she was sitting by an uninteresting

old lady, with whom she was exchanging
occasional quiet remarks; calm and composed,
and, to all appearance, quite unconscious of
his own keen glance, or of a strangely intent
and troubled gaze that she was receiving from
Mr. Max Brendon.

"I was right," said Esher to himself.
"That fellow is in love with her; and what is
more, he heard what I said."

Whether Max Brendon were in love or not,
he was remarkably silent for the rest of the
evening, and took careful note of Esher's and
Magdalen's movements. There was little to
be seen. They kept apart from each other
until it was time to go, and then, when Mr.
St. Aidan took Magdalen to her carriage,
Philip Esher was ready at the door to hand
her in. Further than this Max could not see;
though, if he had been as near as the Rector
was, he would have noticed, as the Rector did
not, that Miss Lingard took no heed of the
proffered hand, and spoke only to Mr. St. Aidan

as she took her seat.   Captain Esher came
back with a dark frown upon his face.

Max said good-night to Mrs. St. Aidan, and
went slowly home with a sense of bewilder-
ment.   He could not believe that Magdalen
cared for Captain Esher; he knew—better
than she could know, he thought—what sort
of a man Philip Esher was.   Surely her
delicate instincts would warn her against him !
And yet there was that eager, impassioned
whisper, " I will sing—*to you*," still ringing
in his ears.   What right had Captain Esher to
sing to Magdalen ?

CHAPTER XI.

THE LAST ATTACK.

CAPTAIN ESHER had not been at the Priory for nearly a week—a wonderful gap in his series of visits. Possibly he thought that a little absence might plead his cause more effectually than words could do. At last, one afternoon about four o'clock, he presented himself in Magdalen's drawing-room, with his hands full of flowers and parcels.

" Will you allow me to share these flowers with you ? " he said to Magdalen, in the tone of one who asks rather than bestows a favour. " You used to be fond of them."

She thanked him carelessly and placed the bouquet on a table as if she did not value it, yet she could not help observing that it was

composed of her favourite flowers; he had
remembered them all these years. Dolly and
Daisy did all the admiration for her : it was
easy enough for her to remain silent.

Captain Esher could scarcely be pleased
with the way in which his gift was received,
but he dared not express any dissatisfaction.
It was something that she took his gift at all.

"And now I have a present for you, fairy,"
ne said, turning to Dolly. "What will you
give me for it ?"

"Kisses," said Dolly.

"I want something better than kisses : I
am tired of kisses."

Dolly pouted.

"I've nothing else to give you, papa."

"We'll see about that," said her father,
smiling. "Catch!" and he threw a parcel
into the air, which Dolly leaped up to seize,
and began to unfasten with eager hands,
uttering exclamations of delight as the con-
tents came to view.

"It's the fan and the sash you promised me: how lovely! Oh, Maidie, I shall wear this with my white frocks! Did they really come from Paris?"

She was unfolding a wonderful fabric of gold-embroidered, rose-coloured silk, made scarf-wise, and a daintily painted, spangled fan, while she spoke. Captain Esher laughed. Magdalen could not forbear a troubled smile as the little creature tied the broad ribbon round her waist and flourished the fan with the air of a miniature princess.

"I must go and look in the big glass upstairs," she said, suddenly, and rushed off, leaving the door wide open.

"A true woman's love of dress!" said Captain Esher, cynically. "You look very grave over it, Magdalen; why should not the child have the privilege of her sex?"

"Rather a failing than a privilege."

"All women are not perfect. I would, on the whole, rather not see my Dolly a saint;

she has not the physique for it. Saints—in
my experience of them, which has been small
—have pale, calm faces, statuesque and a
little cold in repose ; they are tall, majestic,
' beautiful exceedingly.' Dolly is not of that
mould ; she will be a very bewitching little
person, but a woman of the world and a flirt."

"You do not sketch a pleasing picture of
her future," said Magdalen. She was not
much like his portrait of a saint at that
moment, for her face was warmly flushed, her
lips curving with displeasure.

" Don't I ? An attractive one at any rate—
to a man." Magdalen was silent. "Not but
what both pictures have a peculiar charm to
me," he went on ; " for I have now seen them
combined in one person—or, as I should say,
I have seen both represented at successive
stages of life by the same person."

At this minute, the door opened, and Daisy
appeared, carefully carrying a vase in which
she had placed the flowers.

"Come here, Daisy," said Captain Esher, "I was talking about an old friend of mine; would you like to hear about her?"

Daisy put down the vase and said, "Yes, papa." She stood by his knee, but did not offer to climb upon it as Dolly would have done; nor, in his turn, did he try to caress and play with her as he generally did with Dolly.

"She was very proud, this friend of mine," said Philip Esher, his eyes on Magdalen still, "very proud of her truth, and purity, and goodness, but very unmerciful to people who did wrong. She was beautiful and young; she had never been tempted, and she did not know what temptation was. She wanted to be loved alone, and could not bear that her friends' hearts should stray from her a moment. When she found that one of them had for a little while forgotten her, she was offended; and although he was very sorry, she would not speak to him again. Now, what do you think of her, Daisy?"

"I think she was very unkind," said Daisy. "Maidie says we ought to forgive people who offend us."

"Magdalen teaches you that, does she? Well, Daisy, I saw this friend of mine a little while ago. She was more beautiful than ever, though she had grown graver, older, and less joyful. But she was just as hard to her old enemy, and though he begged her to forgive him, she refused. Was she not very cruel?"

"I think so. But——" Daisy hesitated, and looked from her father to Magdalen, "he must have done something very bad. What do *you* think, Maidie?"

"There, there; that will do," said Captain Esher; "go and find Dolly; that is enough."

Half-conscious that she had vexed him in some incomprehensible manner, Daisy sprang away, and he turned round saying, "Well, Magdalen, what do *you* think?"

"Daisy does not understand," was the quiet reply, in the very words that she had used to

Mrs. St. Aidan, "that there are things in the world which a woman has no right to forgive."

"Never? Not if the offender repents?"

"Perhaps upon repentance. But you do not repent, Captain Esher."

There was no contending with that accent of conviction. Captain Esher drummed impatiently upon the table, shrugged his shoulders, and looked far from pleasant. Magdalen really asked too much from him, and he was hardly in the mood to humour her by more lying than was necessary. And as he hesitated what to say or do, the children's voices were heard again, and Dolly entered with her sash and fan, while Daisy followed wistfully behind.

"Papa, haven't you brought a fan or a sash for Daisy?"

"Daisy does not care for such vanities, does she? No; I have nothing else."

"I don't want anything," said Daisy, with

tears in her eyes, but a brave attempt to smile.

Dolly tore off her sash, angrily. "Then I won't have them. There! which will you have? Choose, Daisy."

"Nonsense; you are not to give them away," said Captain Esher. "They are for you, Dolly; you are to keep them."

Magdalen wondered whether it was pure love of torturing that made him say this; for Daisy's tears fell one by one over her cheeks, and Dolly changed to an image of rage incarnate.

"I won't have either of them," she said, and before Magdalen could interfere, had thrown the fan to the other end of the room, and torn the scarf down the middle, then looked with triumphant flashing eyes at her father. Captain Esher uttered his low, teasing laugh, and Dolly would perhaps have flown at him with all the force of her tiny arms, had not two firm hands been placed upon her shoulders. The father laughed again and strode to the window, as he saw Magdalen gather up into her arms the crying, struggling child, and carry her swiftly from the room. Daisy crept after her, and Captain Esher was left alone, though for some minutes he heard the shrieking sobs that resounded through the passage as the child was borne away.

When all was quiet, Magdalen came back, with a firm tread, and shining, resolute eyes. She waited by the table as if composing herself to speak, and in the interval Esher said in his lazy, mischievous tones—

" There 's some devil in that child."

" The devil that tempts her is outside, I think," said Magdalen, looking him full in the face.

" You flatter me, Madge ? "

" A stop must be put to all this, Captain Esher."

" I am sure I have no objection," said

Esher, contemplating his filbert-shaped nails with great interest. " Might I ask what is to be stopped ? "

" These scenes in which you try to arouse all the evil nature in your children," said Magdalen. " You bribed me into receiving you into my house by promising that Dolly and Daisy should stay unharmed, while you were allowed to visit them. I thought they would be happy and safe with me; but I think now that they would be better anywhere else, so long as your whole object is to undo my work and weaken my influence. We must change our plans; I see it is not right for you to be in my house."

" What ! you propose to prevent my seeing Dolly and Daisy ? "

" I wish I could! I know that it is impossible. You must please think of me as the children's schoolmistress, who has some right to demand that their life shall not be constantly disturbed by their father's cruel fondness. I have certainly a right to limit your visits, Captain Esher."

"And the father has a right to take his children away from the school where the mistress is so severe," said Esher, emphasising his words.

" Of course."

" I don't wonder at your getting tired of them," he went on, slowly. "Dolly is a perfect little fury at times; and Daisy is decidedly uninteresting. Besides, they are *not* your own children. 'The patience of the saints,' of which I have somewhere heard, might well fail with them. They had better come away with me."

Magdalen's face paled, but she did not speak.

"Let our quarrel be settled in another way," said Captain Esher, coming round to her side, "and then I will do my best to become an exemplary father to those two girls, or, at any rate, I will leave them

entirely to your care. You say you cannot
forgive me; well, be it so; you may find out
some day that you have helped to make me a
better man than you took me for; but think of
the children, and finish your work with them
if you want to do good, Magdalen. Be their
mother in earnest; come and make a home
for them at Malton; I swear to you that I
will never interfere with what you think best
for them. You know what guidance they
need; I will trust them entirely in your
hands; only come!"

"To be your wife!"

He was chilled by the tone of shuddering
dismay in which she spoke, but proceeded
rapidly—

"Yes, Magdalen, to be my wife—and their
mother. We will not talk about love, nor
of those past sins which you say you cannot
forgive; let me but remind you of the good
you would do my children, of the dangers
from which your example and teaching

will preserve them.   Remember that if
you refuse me, you must say good-bye to
them.   We cannot go on as we have been
doing lately—it is an unnatural state of
things; and I cannot give up my children
entirely to you; you must take all of us or
none."

"None," she said, in a dull, sad tone, a
mere echo of his own.   He went on, however:

"You are cruel to them if you refuse.   Can
a religious woman like you neglect so splendid
an opportunity of doing good?"   She shrank
at the sneering tone, and he changed it for a
more earnest one.   "Magdalen, I mean it!
If you have any love for them, come and be
their mother."

He tried to read some answer in her face,
but it was turned away from him, and the
attitude in which she had sunk down was
one of intense dejection.

He stood close beside her, longing to take
her in his arms, but not daring to touch her

until she gave him leave. She had some power over him still; more power than she dreamed of, more than he would have acknowledged even to himself.

"Magdalen," he said, "have you no love left for *me?*"

"No, no," she cried, starting as if she had been stung; "I have none—for you—for anybody. Oh, leave me, Philip, I cannot bear any more."

The utterance of his name gave him courage.

"My darling," he said, "you need a helper. Let me help you; let me love you. After all our troubles, let us learn to be happy together. No one will ever love you as I do, Magdalen; and you gave the first love of your heart to me many years ago."

His voice was musical, his manner tender and impassioned. But his words touched other chords than those which he had meant to reach. She stood up, wearily stroking the hair back from her forehead, and averting her face from his eager glance. But still she did not speak.

"I will not ask you for an answer now," he said, with great tact. "I will come again— in two or three days—on Monday, perhaps, when you have thought over the matter. I could plead for my own sake; but I will not. I will ask you only to think of the children, Magdalen, and what you might be to them."

Thus he left her, and when Magdalen was alone she covered her face with her hands and wept bitterly.

For the next two or three days, Captain Esher left her in peace. She was glad to be free of him—glad to be alone, free even of the children's company. It was plain that he had managed to give the two little girls some idea of the state of the case. Dolly and Daisy seemed to her to look at her with strange, considering eyes. Both children were almost oppressively loving and submissive—so sweet and good, indeed, as to make Magdalen's heart contract from time to time with a violent pang of grief at the very thought of letting them go away from her. How should she live without them?

She was strongly tempted to do evil that good might come. For very evil in her eyes was this proposed marriage with Philip Esher. And yet she was almost ready to take the risk. The children were so very dear to her! And the consciousness that she would then be choosing a dangerous course by no means deprived it of fascination. Magdalen had less of the saint than the woman about her still.

Sunday found her still undecided. It rained, and she did not go to church in the evening, but read aloud to the children, servants, and customary visitors until half-past seven. Then she settled herself in her sitting-room with Daisy on her lap, and Dolly silently leaning her head against her knee.

"Papa hasn't been here all day," said Daisy.

"He won't come till to-morrow," responded Dolly, in an odd, abrupt way. "He said that Magdalen would perhaps let him come. then."

Dolly scarcely ever used the old abbreviation "Maidie" now. Captain Esher did not like .it, and she copied him in his likes and dislikes as much as possible.

"Will you let him come, Maidie?" whispered Daisy, stroking Magdalen's face.

"I don't know, Daisy."

"Do, Maidie."

Magdalen sighed. Dolly sat up and looked round.

"Cousin Magdalen, don't you want to marry papa?"

"Hush, Dolly, hush; you don't know what you say."

"Yes, I do; papa told me. He made me promise that I would be good if you did.

And I will be good, Magdalen, if you will marry papa, for he wants you so much."

"You would be our mamma then," said Daisy, wistfully; "and that would be so nice. Let me call you mamma, dear Maidie."

"My children, hush, you do not know," cried Magdalen, rising in her agitation, and putting Daisy aside: "you must not speak in that way. I cannot listen to you."

The children were silenced, but Magdalen's heart spoke louder than before.

When they had gone to bed, she sat for some time over the fire in her little sitting-room, thinking of the answer that she was to give to Philip Esher on the morrow. It was strange that she could not decide. Her heart drew her one way, her conscience another, and between the two opposing influences Magdalen sorrowfully acknowledged that her will was weak. A touch might decide her either way: which should it be?

A light knock at the door roused her from

her meditations. To her extreme surprise, Ursula Brendon suddenly entered the room and closed the door behind her. She was a frequent visitor at the Priory, but she had never before presented herself at this late hour on a Sunday night. Magdalen noticed at once that there was something a little odd in her demeanour. Her face was flushed, her eyes shone, her breath came thick and fast as if she had been running, her short curly hair was wet with rain, and her ulster and hat were dripping.

"My dear child," said Magdalen, "come to the fire and take off your coat. You will be wet through."

But, to her surprise, Ursula gently forced her back into her chair, and then cast herself down on her knees before her and looked up into her face.

"Tell me that it's not true!" she panted. "Oh, do say that it isn't true."

"That what is not true?"

"You are not going to marry that man? that Mr. Esher!—Oh, Magdalen, do hear me," cried the girl, as Magdalen made a slight movement as if to rise; "for pity's sake, listen to me, for I am sure you do not know!"

"Do not know what?" said Magdalen compelling herself to speak more calmly than she felt.

"You do not know what sort of a man he is! Oh, please don't be angry with me, Magdalen. I could not bear it: I ran away from home to tell you, because I am so miserable about it. And I am sure you would not be happy if you had to give up your classes at Gay Street, and your poor people, and turn Miss Jessop and everybody into the street——"

"Ursula this is madness!"

"No, it isn't, indeed, Magdalen, dear. And Max knows it isn't, too, only of course he could not say a word. You know how much he cares for you!—more than all the world beside—or perhaps you don't know; but *I* know, and some day you will know too——"

"I cannot listen to this, Ursula."

"No; and I won't say a word more about Max, dear Magdalen; but only let me tell you what I heard about Captain Esher. Indeed, indeed, I think that you ought to hear."

And Magdalen listened with tingling pulses and flaming cheeks, while Ursula told her tale.

CHAPTER XII.

MAGDALEN'S DECISION.

" It was Cecil who told us," said Ursula, in her headlong, impetuous way. " He came in with us from church this evening, and he said that he was at the Conservative Club Rooms last night—you know the place, in Enfield Street —and Captain Esher was there, and some of the gentlemen were talking to him—' chaffing him,' Cecil called it, in his horrid slangy way —about the rich woman he was going to marry—that was *you*, Magdalen, you know— and about your having turned the Priory into a hospital and an orphanage (do forgive me for saying it, dear), and Captain Esher laughed and said——"

" Ursula, I do not wish to hear what he said.
228

You have no business to come to me with these stories."

"You shall not go! you must hear!" cried Ursula, catching at Magdalen's hands, and forcibly detaining her while she hurriedly continued her recital;—"and Captain Esher laughed and said, 'Oh, there'll soon be an end to that when she's my wife. I shall turn the whole set of pensioners out of doors, and send the kids to a French convent-school, while we spend our time at Vienna or Paris: I'll stand no preaching, I can tell you.' And everybody laughed, and Cecil said that Captain Esher had been drinking too much—that he was 'half seas over,' or something of that kind."

Magdalen had extricated herself from Ursula's grasp by this time and walked to the other end of the room. The girl had never seen her look so angry.

"And you came up here to bring me this gossip," she said, in a tone that cut Ursula to the heart.

"If you call it gossip," she began, choking back the sob that rose in her throat, and then stopping short to regain her self-possession. "I thought that you ought to know. It is all quite true : Cecil heard it, and Max heard it too, for he tried to make Cecil be quiet, and said that it was no business of mine when I asked him straight out whether Captain Esher had said so. But he looked so black that I was sure it was true; and he couldn't deny it!"

"And you came here to enlighten my mind?" said Magdalen, with a touch of satire in her voice.

"I thought that you ought to know," Ursula repeated, stubbornly. "Nobody knows that I have come; they are all at supper. Magdalen, you won't—you *won't* marry Captain Esher?"

"My dear Ursula," said Miss Lingard, gravely but gently—she had recovered from her momentary vexation of spirit,—"I think that you should not ask me that question. As your brother remarked, it is really not your business." But she smiled a little as she spoke. "Now, I am sorry not to be able to keep you, but you must go home immediately. I will send one of the servants with you. Just think what anxiety your mother will be feeling if she finds that you are not in the house! How can you do these wild things, dear child?"

Ursula submitted to be reproved, and then very tenderly kissed before she was sent away under the convoy of a couple of maid-servants. But she did not yield her point. At the very last moment, as she clung round Magdalen's neck and said good-bye, she managed to whisper another sentence into her friend's reluctant ear: "You won't give up all your work, and turn your poor people adrift, will you, Magdalen?" And Magdalen's "Don't be foolish, child," had not a reassuring sound in Ursula's ear.

Magdalen returned to her meditations with the sense of having had a mental shock. With a little touch of perversity she refused at first to acknowledge that Ursula's words had had any effect upon her. " I will not heed gossip," she said to herself, resolutely. " I will not believe even of Philip Esher that he would speak of me in that way before his friends— nay, before strangers, for he does not know the Brendons; never in his right mind would he have forgotten himself so much!" Then Ursula's words about Philip's state of semi-intoxication recurred to her, and made her shiver with disgust. " Is it possible ? Has he sunk so low ? No ; I will not believe that it is true. And yet—and yet—" again she thought of Ursula's disjointed sentences—" Max could not deny it. Max looked so black that I was sure it was true." " Max Brendon would never allow a report to be circulated in his presence unless there were some foundation for it. He could not contradict it ; and he had heard it

all. Ah, then, it must be true." Such was
Magdalen's involuntary conclusion, and she
blushed as she formulated it. Why should
she trust Max Brendon so implicitly? It was
no use questioning herself; she did trust him,
and that was enough. In her heart of hearts
she knew that she believed Ursula's story.

It came across her with sudden and strange
distinctness that she and Philip Esher lived
in two separate worlds. There was surely no
need for any one to tell her that he would
oppose her schemes for good; that he would
scoff at her benevolence, and scatter her
charitable projects to the winds! Could she
imagine him at the Priory, amongst her pale
seamstresses, her infirm old women, her
rickety children from the London slums?
He would never be content with anything but
the gayest, brightest, most exciting of worldly
lives. He would dispose of the children (as
he had said) in some fashionable school, and
he would take wing to the most frequented

resort of Europe—the most pleasure-loving cities, the wildest rounds of dissipation and indulgence. It seemed to Magdalen that she might have known this all along—that her hesitation had been a madness which might have hurled her to uttermost destruction! What had she been thinking of? Ally herself to Philip Esher, who feared neither God nor man, who spared neither young nor old, woman nor child, in the furtherance of his own designs? Did Miss Esher leave her the Priory for this end? And—higher and more solemn question—had God given her wealth and position and responsibility in order that she might please herself by keeping two little children in her care, at any cost? No, not even for Dolly and Daisy could she do this thing. She did not love Philip Esher; and she would never marry a man whom she did not love. Her mind was made up: she would do the thing that was right, and leave the result to God.

Before she went to bed that night she wrote her letter to Philip Esher. She refused his offer of marriage, unconditionally. She begged leave to keep his children with her still; but she also said that not even for their sakes would she change her decision. She had no love to give him, and she would not marry without love.

Captain Esher received this note in the course of the following afternoon, and could not believe the evidence of his eyes in reading it. He walked up to the Priory in a state of intense though suppressed fury, and was met at the door with the information, from the lips of an old servant, that the children had gone into the country for a few days with Miss Jessop. Magdalen had no thought of keeping them from their father for more than a day or two; but it had seemed to her better to put them out of his way until the violence of his anger against her should have abated.

"I should like to see Miss Lingard," said Esher, on receiving this intelligence. "Take her my card, and say I particularly wish to speak to her."

"I can't do that, sir, begging your pardon. I was ordered not to admit you if you came."

Captain Esher looked daggers at old Becky in her clean white cap, and exclaimed as she was on the point of closing the door, in a voice nearly stiffled with passion—

"Wait! The children's address!"

Without speaking, Becky immediately held out to him a card with an address upon it, written in Magdalen's clear handwriting. It was plain that she had expected him to come. While he looked at it and hesitated for a moment, the old servant, who knew the state of affairs quite as well as he did, and hated him cordially, took the opportunity of quietly shutting the door in his face. It was of no use to protest: he was alone on the broad stone steps, with that solid door before him;

and in spite of his rage and baffled hopes Captain Esher saw that his only wisdom lay in retreat. But he was not inclined to give up a last chance that remained to him. Magdalen might possibly be going down to Gay Street between seven and eight o'clock, and he might intercept her and force from her the reason for this treatment of him. It was six o'clock now : not very long to wait.

Mr. St. Aidan was much astonished to find that no Magdalen appeared for her class that evening. She was generally there at seven on Mondays, but at five minutes to eight, when he arrived, there was a little crowd of inquiring girls at the door—and no Miss Lingard.

"I can't think what has become of Miss Lingard," he said to Max. "She is generally so punctual that I am afraid something is wrong. I wish I knew what to do."

"I'll run up and see, if you like. My class doesn't begin till half-past eight. I can get to the Priory and back in half-an-hour."

Mr. St. Aidan hesitated, objected, but finally gave way to Max's determination, and saw him go. He had time to grow uneasy and a little indignant before his coadjutor returned.

Max walked rapidly up the hill to Higher Scarsfield, and reached Miss Lingard's house by ten minutes past eight. At the gate he stopped to look at his watch. He put back the watch in his pocket, and noticed that the figure of a man stood in the shade given by some overhanging lilac and elder-bushes hanging over the garden wall. He looked hard at the figure, but could not recognise it. But no sooner had he entered the gate and rung the door-bell than Captain Esher crept slowly out of the shadow and watched the new-comer through the gate.

The door was opened. Max did not go in, but stood for several minutes on the door-step—evidently while the servant took some message to Miss Lingard. Captain Esher

opened the gate and stole a little nearer.
There was Magdalen herself! Magdalen, who
had declared she could see no visitors! She
was talking to this young man, who, only a
week ago, Esher had declared was in love
with her. A bold stroke was necessary: for
very shame Magdalen could not refuse to
speak to him now. He advanced from the
shade of the shrubbery, and stood at the very
foot of the steps. Magdalen stopped speaking,
and turned pale. Max, whose back was to
Captain Esher, wheeled round and saw
him.

"Your servant informed me that you could
not see visitors," he said, lifting his hat with
ironical politeness, and showing that his face
was deeply flushed. "I find that she was
mistaken : *some* visitors are received."

His tone was so insolent that Max thought
that he had been drinking, and stood so that
Esher could not easily pass him on the steps
unless Miss Lingard asked him to advance.

"If you can see *him*, you can see me," said Esher.

"Stop!" said Max, barring his progress. "No farther, unless Miss Lingard invites you, sir."

"I do not invite him," Magdalen answered, clearly. "I have already refused you admittance to-night, Captain Esher; I am surprised that you cannot see how unwelcome your presence is."

"Out of the way, you fool!" said Esher, adding a strong epithet as he tried ineffectually to push by Max. "I will see her, I tell you—she'll be my wife some day——"

"Is that true, Miss Lingard?" asked Max, without yielding an inch of ground.

"No; and never will be true," said Magdalen.

"Then the sooner you are off this lady's premises the better," said Max, sharply, as he became more and more convinced that the man was half-intoxicated, "or I shall give you in charge."

Captain Esher threw his cigar into Max's face. There was a momentary struggle, serious though silent, between the two men; then Philip Esher was seen falling down the steps, frantically catching at the iron railing as he went. Magdalen uttered a faint cry.

But he was not seriously hurt. He gathered himself together, lifted his head, brushed the dust from his knees, and rose to his feet again.

"I suppose I must accept that dismissal," he said, with a sneer, rendered more ugly than usual by the sudden ghastly whiteness of his face, and a bleeding cut upon one temple. "I shall not forget it, Miss Lingard; and as for you, Mr. Max Brendon, you'll pay for it sooner or later. I shall remember *you*."

He turned smartly upon his heel, and walked away without once looking round.

"I beg your pardon, Miss Lingard," said Max. "I could hardly help myself. He would have been inside the house in another moment."

Magdalen's face was pale, but she tried to smile. The effort was too great, however: after a short, sharp struggle with herself she turned away and covered her eyes with her hand. Max hesitated for a moment, then entered the house and closed the door behind him.

" It has been too much for you," he said, in a low tone, as they stood together in the dimly lighted hall. " Will you not rest now? And will you pardon my violence ?"

For answer, she gave him her hand. Max took it in both his own, and then, acting on an impulse which seemed to him uncontrollable, he bent his head and kissed it. Magdalen started, but could not speak. And before she had recovered her self-command he was gone. The little act of homage was his farewell.

Magdalen sat down on one of the old carved chairs in the hall, her hands pressed tightly together, her head bent. A rush of actual fear had come across her. For the first time she seemed to know of what Philip Esher was capable when his wrath was aroused. She had roused it now most effectually—she and Max Brendon together. What would be the upshot of it all? For that he would try to revenge himself upon them both she was but too well assured.

For herself, she knew what to expect. She had sent the children to a friend's house in the country with Miss Jessop, because she had been certain that their father's anger would be almost ungovernable in the first hours of his mortification and disappointment. He would not care what he said in their presence—how he reviled her and wounded her through them. It would be better, she thought, that, for a few hours at least, they should be out of the way. He could not see them until the next day, and by that time his anger might have cooled. He would probably take them away from her and send them to school—but that

she could not help.   Not even for them would
Magdalen consent to sell her own soul.

And the other person on whom Philip
would be eager to revenge himself? What
would be the effect of this night's work on
Max Brendon's prospects? A lawsuit was
already pending between him and Captain
Esher; it might be taken for granted that it
would now be pushed forward with vigour.
Neither of the combatants would allow it to
drop, after what had passed between them
that night on Magdalen's door-step. She did
not know whether the issues involved were
great or small, but she felt sure that Max
Brendon would suffer every annoyance and
injury that Philip was able to inflict. She
wondered whether Captain Esher would take
out a summons for assault against Max; as he
was himself the aggressor it was hardly likely
that he would do so, except for pure spite and
the desire to give Magdalen the annoyance of
appearing as a witness. For this last reason,

however, it was quite possible that he would sacrifice his own repute in the attempt to bring trouble on the heads of other people.

Seeing him in this light, Magdalen shuddered to think of the danger that she had run. She remembered with shrinking awe that not long ago she had felt uncertain as to whether her old love for Philip might not yet revive. She had feared to meet him lest she should find her heart once more in his keeping. That had been the real explanation of her dislike to his visits, her desire to avoid his presence. She had been very near falling into the snare. If Philip had had a little more prudence, a little more self-control, she would have believed in his repentance and in his love for her. He had himself undone his own work as fast as it was achieved. His treatment of the children, his sneers at her faith and her charities, had displayed his real character too clearly for her to misunderstand it any longer. She was certain now, more certain than she could ever have been before, that her love for Philip Esher was gone, and gone for ever.

In the background of her mind she still heard Ursula repeating some words to which she was resolved that she would give no attention. "You know how much Max cares for you. He will tell you so some day." What folly Ursula talked! It had been wrong to listen to her; it was wrong to think of what she said. And yet—as if to corroborate the girl's words, there came to Magdalen's mind the memory of the kiss softly pressed upon her hand that evening. Were Ursula's words true? Could it be possible that Max Brendon "cared" for her—loved her as a man should love a woman, "better than all the world beside"? And if so, what then? Magdalen could not tell.

CHAPTER XIII.

ALONE.

DURING the dark hours of the night and in the intervals of business in the course of the next day, Max had leisure to think a good deal about Miss Lingard. He almost wondered at his own temerity when he remembered how he had taken leave of her; and it was with an odd thrill of the nerves that he reflected on the fact that she had shown no anger, no resentment; that the little start of astonishment which she had given when his lips came in contact with her hand alone showed that she was conscious of his caress. This unpremeditated action of his—this momentary touch of her soft, warm hand with his mouth—had stimulated his passion to a

surprising extent. She had long attracted
him : he had been haunted by her sweet face
and musical tones for many a day ; but it
was only of late that he had discovered what
this fascination meant. The latent passion
in him leaped up like a long-smouldered
flame that at last has found a vent. He
knew now that his affection for Lenore, and
even for the faithless jilt who had played
with him in his boyhood, had been " as
moonlight unto sunlight, and as water unto
wine," compared with his present love. With
all the strength and fervour of his manhood,
he had given his love to Magdalen, and to
Magdalen alone. And for the first time he
realised, with a quickening of his pulses, that
it was possible, since she had not been offended
when he kissed her hand, that she was not
entirely indifferent to him.

Ursula's escapade had, fortunately for her,
passed unnoticed. She had managed to slip
out of the house unobserved. It was thought

that she had gone to bed, as she had been
complaining of a headache earlier in the day,
and nobody had thought of going in to inquire after her welfare. She re-entered the
house by the side-door, ·and fled upstairs at
once without encountering anybody; and,
although the servants grumbled next day at
finding her ulster and dress and hat in a
damp, crumpled heap upon her bedroom floor,
none of them thought of reporting the circumstance, or even of wondering how she
had managed to make herself so wet.

Max was annoyed to find that his mother
had heard some gossip about Miss Lingard
and Captain Esher, and was bent upon putting
him through an examination upon it.

" Really, mother," he said at last, rising
from his chair with a displeased look, " I
cannot see why I should be expected to know
more than other people about Miss Lingard
and Captain Esher."

" You might know something, considering

your connection with the St. Aidans. Tell
us this: do you know whether they are engaged?" asked Gertrude.

"Yes, I do know; but I think they do not
want their affairs to be gossiped about," he
answered rather severely.

"If they have told *you*, their affairs can
be no great secret," said Mrs. Brendon.

"Ah, well; true. Well, I suppose it does
not much signify," said Max, taking up a
book. "All the world says that they are
not engaged, and I think I may say that all
the world is right."

"Do you know anything more?"

"No."

"Haven't you asked Miss Lingard to
marry you yet?" Mrs. Brendon asked,
satirically.

"No."

"May I ask if you mean to do so?"

"I'll wait till I have done it before I tell
anybody," said Max, getting up with a smile.

To treat the matter lightly was the only way of concealing his vexation.

He made his way into the hall and was putting on his coat when Ursula stopped him, her face full of excitement and eagerness.

"Max, Max, how do you know?"

"How do I know what?"

"That Magdalen is not going to marry Captain Esher."

"I heard her say so," said Max, shortly.

Ursula gave a light little bound into the air. "Oh, I am so glad! Then she did believe what I told her."

"What *you* told her?" Max turned upon his sister with as much severity as voice and manner could possibly express. "What do you mean?"

"You won't betray me, I know," said Ursula, fearlessly. "I went up to the Priory on Sunday night and told her all that Cecil had been saying."

She had never seen Max look so stern.

"Ursula, you do not know the mischief you might do by your indiscriminate meddling with other people's affairs. We shall be afraid to speak before you soon. You do not deserve to be trusted."

A year ago Ursula would have pouted, or been defiant; now she only laughed.

"Dearest Max, you do look so very grim! I told her a good deal more than that. Do you think I don't know your secret?"

"Do you mean that you had the audacity——"

"I only dropped a word by accident, Max. I only said that you thought more of her than all the world beside, or something to that effect. She'll never think of it again."

"You had no business to say anything about either my feelings or her affairs."

"So she told me," said Ursula, saucily. "I won't say anything more;—having said all I wanted," she added to herself.

Max was not mollified. He muttered something excessively uncomplimentary respecting Ursula's discretion—or want of it —as he went out, but as it was less severe than she expected, or indeed ˙ deserved, she thought that she had got off very cheaply.

He was on his way to Gay Street. Mr. St. Aidan was not to be there, and Max had his own and the Rector's work to do. He did not think that Miss Lingard would be present; he knew that she must still be deeply disturbed by the events of the previous night, and expected to find that she had sent an excuse; but, to his surprise, she was in her usual place, and at her usual work. He was so much accustomed to find that the slightest shadow of uneasiness or illness would keep his mother and elder sister from their ordinary duties, that he had unconsciously judged Magdalen by them, and had to acknowledge to himself

with a smile, half proud, half pleased, that
she—the woman whom he loved—was not
to be judged by common standards, and that
to her, duty came before personal pleasure
or convenience.

He made haste to be at the door when
she came out, and asked if he might not
walk home with her, as Mr. St. Aidan was
not there.

She hesitated for a moment, and he
thought that he saw a slight flush rise to
her cheeks. Then she assented very graci-
ously, with a smile the sweetness of which
intoxicated him, giving him a sense of courage and hope that he had never felt
before.

The night was dark, but fine; the old
church clock struck ten as they left the
door. Max offered her his arm; she took
it, after a moment's hesitation; and it was
the touch of her hand that kept him silent
for a time, thinking, in spite of reason

and common sense, of the joy and comfort it would be to him to have her always beside him, always to see her as the guiding star, the beacon of his hitherto somewhat gloomy life.

Magdalen spoke first.

"Can you tell me," she said, rather falteringly, "whether Captain Esher is still in Scarsfield or not?"

"I believe not, Miss Lingard. I heard, by chance, that he left the town this morning."

"I was half afraid," she said, in a very low voice, "that I might see him—to-night—when I walked home——"

"And yet you came! You are brave," said Max, his voice tenderer than he knew.

"Oh, no," she answered, "I am a great coward. I am afraid now."

"Of what?"

"Of *him*. Not for myself, exactly; for

others—for you. He never forgives—never forgets."

Max felt a mad longing to kiss the little hand that lay so lightly on his arm. But he restrained himself, and answered, quietly,

" I assure you, Miss Lingard, he can do me no harm. I am not afraid of him."

" But there is a lawsuit likely to come on, is there not! About your chemical works and their effect on his property ?"

" Yes. But a private quarrel will make no difference. I am much more seriously concerned lest he should annoy you again. If there is anything that I can do, any way in which I can help you——"

" Thank you, Mr. Brendon. I am only afraid of one thing for myself. He can take the children away from me ; he threatened to do it long ago. I am afraid of that."

" It is a mean and cruel way of taking his revenge," said Max, warmly.

"It is cruel," she responded, sadly, "but he is not a man from whom one can expect mercy. He knows that I love his children; that fact gives him power which he would not otherwise have had."

Max felt a throb of pleasure at these words. She was condescending to explain to him why she had tolerated Captain Esher so long.

"He may perhaps remember all that you have done for them," he said, searching for something that would comfort her.

She shook her head.

"He will remember nothing," she answered, drearily, "except that he has been offended, and that the person who offended him must be made to suffer."

"You will suffer. You will be left alone," said Max, hurriedly.

"Yes." She sighed as she said the word. "I shall be left alone."

Max lost his head. He had made up his mind what to say, and had intended to put his meaning very plainly and yet in a very reasonable manner: but at the supreme moment, his carefully prepared sentences went completely out of his mind. If he spoke like a blundering school-boy, his love was to blame rather than his judgment; and Magdalen, with her sore heart, was not disposed to judge him harshly.

"There is one who would give all the world to prevent your feeling sad or lonely any more. If only I could comfort you a little! If it would be any good to you to know that I think there is no other woman like you— that I love you with my whole heart—I ask for no other recompense; I only care to make you, if possible, a little happier."

She had withdrawn her hand from his arm, and paused in the dark road which they were traversing. He could not see her face distinctly, but, somehow, he knew that she was trembling.

"Don't let me trouble you," he went on.

"I ask for nothing that you do not wish to give. Only—if ever I can help you—if ever you want a friend or a helper, I am here, always ready. I dare not ask for more than your friendship—your trust; but you shall know, once and for all, that I love you, and always shall love you, to the last days of my life."

His tone was dogged in its determination. Her silence afforded him no hope. Her very attitude seemed to give him the answer that he had dreaded; it was an attitude of doubt, almost of fear.

"Mr. Brendon," she said at last, and her tone was one of distress, "I do not know what to say."

"There is no need to beat about the bush," he said, still doggedly: "tell me at once that you do not love me, that there is no hope for me, and send me about my business. I know that I had no right to aspire to you; it was presumption on my part."

"No," said Magdalen, in a firmer voice, "I do not think that. And yet I cannot tell you to—to—hope, as you phrase it. I do not intend to marry. I have my work."

"And is there anything in a marriage with me that would prevent your doing your work?" he asked.

"I cannot think of it," she said, still distressfully. "Don't urge me; don't ask me. I do not feel as if I could ever love—again."

The last word came out very low, almost inaudibly; but Max caught it. He started, and kept silence. He had forgotten that she had loved a man like Philip Esher; so different in every way from himself. Memories of the old story of her engagement came back to him. No doubt, after all, she loved Philip Esher still! He was a fool.

The two were still standing on the road. Now Magdalen moved on.

"Forgive me if I hurt you," she said, gently but very firmly. "I did not mean to mislead you — if I have misled you — in the past. I have had my love-history and outlived it. I will not marry any man unless I love him."

"And you do not love me? How should you?—I understand."

They walked on silently for some little time. Max's heart was full of grief, trouble, and bitterness; Magdalen's pulses throbbed with a strange pain, a strange uncertainty. In a faltering voice she said at last,

"Let us be friends still, Mr. Brendon. Let us forget what you have said. You can often help and advise me; I shall be so glad of your friendship." In her heart she said, "I cannot do without your friendship." But as yet she scarcely recognised that still small voice.

"I have said that is all I ask," Max answered, sadly. "If my friendship is of any use to you, I shall feel honoured. If ever you want more than friendship from me, it is yours. Call on me when you will, for what you will."

"If ever I need you," said Magdalen, gravely, "I will not forget what you have said. Here is my hand on it, Mr. Brendon. We are friends still."

They had reached the garden gate. He walked with her up the drive towards the front door, which, to their surprise, was standing half-open. Magdalen quickened her steps as she advanced. A flood of light streamed from the hall; a hum of voices was heard; the place, to their eyes, wore an unwonted aspect.

"What can be wrong?" Max heard her rather breathe than speak.

"My dear," said old Becky, meeting her at the door, "we 've had a loss, and you will feel it sorely. Bear up, my dear; it 'll all come right at last."

Magdalen turned deathly pale.

"The children! Are they here—here? Let me see them!"

"Madge, dear Madge," said Miss Jessop,

throwing herself tearfully into Magdalen's arms, "it was not my fault indeed! Oh, they are quite well, but their father came and said they should never see you again—cruel things he said of you; and he has taken them away to France, I don't know where."

"Taken them—already?"

"Taken them, saying they should never enter Scarsfield again, nor he either; and no one to take care of them except a servant," wailed Miss Jessop.

"This is very sudden," said Magdalen, turning round to Max with the ghost of a smile upon her white lips. "I thought at least I should be able to say good-bye. I am left alone indeed."

"Let me help you; what can I do?" said Max, thrilled with the sight of her sorrow as he had never been in her calmness. "I will bring them back to you."

"No, that you cannot do." She leaned against the wall as though for support and put her hands across her eyes. "It is hard—God's will be done!"

"There, there, she'll be better now," said Becky, seeing the tears well out from under those full eyelids. "All we can do is to let her alone now. Good-night, sir."

Max could not take the hint without saying another word. "Is there nothing I can do for you?" he said, earnestly.

"Nothing."

"Then good-night."

Her hand was stretched out to him, but she could not speak. He held it until Becky's keen glance warned him to desist, and then went out reluctantly into the night. It was hard to leave her alone in her sorrow and to know that she had none to comfort her.

CHAPTER XIV.

"NOT EASILY JEALOUS."

EIGHTEEN months changed the aspect of affairs very little. No great event transpired at any one of the three houses with which our story is concerned. If any change of relations had been brought about amongst the inmates of these dwellings, it took its rise from deeper sources than those of outward circumstance.

Magdalen Lingard was still separated from the children, who were with their father in France. Her rejection of Philip Esher had caused a slight diminution of the friendship between herself and Mrs. St. Aidan, and Magdalen missed the old kindly intercourse very keenly. She threw herself, heart and soul, into work among the poor; but she had never been more lonely, seldom more depressed, than in the long months that followed upon the departure of Dolly and Daisy Esher. There was a blank in her life : she put it down to the children's absence, although at times a suspicion crossed her mind that there was another reason for that sense of aching emptiness.

Lenore and Cecil Brendon lived tranquilly at Chalgrove; but the tranquillity was not altogether unbroken. It was a difficult thing for her to pay constant attention to Cecil's whims and fancies—and these were not few—when she herself was far from strong in health, and her baby fretful and delicate. A drive or a walk with him was a matter of dread to her; for, although he was anxious not to over-tire her, he made his excursions thoughtlessly long, and hated to be reminded of her fatigue. She neither liked to shorten his walks nor to refuse to accompany him, though she would have shown greater kindness and real wisdom in doing so. But at present her sole idea of married life was that the wife should be a devoted slave; and the husband, a noble generous master. She found it easy to play the first rôle—easy, so far as feeling was concerned, for it was an arduous one in fact; the difficulty of her view lay in exalting Cecil to a sufficiently high standpoint. He was given to small worries, petty outbreaks of temper, that somewhat impaired the heroic qualities with which his wife would fain have invested him; and when she wanted to sum up his virtues (which she did sometimes in a spirit of extenuating tenderness rather than in exultant pride), she was apt to decline rapidly from moral qualities to an enumeration of his tastes and hobbies : his love of the beautiful, in house, garden, or personal surroundings, his preference of French over English cookery, and his delight in old china. He was fond of his wife and child, with a sort of condescending fondness : he seemed not to have forgotten his own surprise at himself for loving anybody so well; and it was evident that he had never thrown his whole being into his love—never known what it was to lose sight of his own aims and wishes in care for any other person. Cecil was, in every respect, a half-hearted man; when he spoke, he spoke with an *arrière pensée;* when he felt, he was not sure of the depth or lastingness of his feelings; when he thought, he seldom arrived at definite conclusions, or saw one side of an argument more clearly than another. As if to counterbalance this natural indecision, he occasionally acted with an impetuosity that had its rise in utter fatigue of his own weakness.

These characteristics were not easily understood by Lenore. She herself was peculiarly sincere and truthful; her standard of womanly duty, if not very advanced, was one that she was always trying to attain. She had never tampered with her instincts of right and wrong. When she knew her duty, her impulse was to do it, rather than to find reasons for not doing it. Duty and authority had never, so far, been recognised as possibly opposing elements. In her girlhood she had imagined that duty would some day be embodied to her in the person of a husband, in obeying whom she was sure of doing right. It did not occur to her that her husband might require care, watchfulness, support, from herself. When she longed to rouse Cecil to a better life before her marriage, she imagined that such an awakening could be accomplished at a stroke and once for all. His strong religious feeling, manifested upon his recovery from illness, caused her to believe that this work was done : that her hero was now perfected. From this dream there came a speedy awakening.

The changes that eighteen months had wrought in Ursula Brendon were chiefly for the better. She was handsomer, cleverer, and

—to her mother's surprise—sweeter-tempered than she had ever been before. She still worked hard at her books, but not under the guidance of Miss Quittenden. Ursula was emancipated from the schoolroom: she was " out," and it was not thought worth while to keep an expensive governess for Bessie's sake alone. It was clear that Bessie had not the strength for hard study : she had grown paler and weaker every month so long as Miss Quittenden held sway in the schoolroom. Mrs. Brendon began to see that the child was over-worked; and as soon as Ursula left the schoolroom, she consented to dismiss Miss Quittenden and give Bessie holiday. The respite came a little too late for Bessie's health ; she had developed a spinal affection which had been increased by the want of rest, and it was feared that she would be an invalid for life. Ursula was wonderfully patient with the crossness and irritability which the child could not help showing now and then, and the whole family seemed relieved at the absence of that somewhat too rigid censor of manners and morals, Miss Quittenden.

Max bore about with him a quiet face but a harassed spirit. He had troubles at home in the shape of his mother's captious fault-findings; and greater ones abroad in his money-perplexities. Darley's Chemical Works would pay well in a few years, if he had capital enough to bear a yearly loss until certain of his own improvements and inventions began to be appreciated; in the meantime the drain on his resources was severe. He contributed a sum to the housekeeping arrangements at home; but Mrs. Brendon was an extravagant manager, and he was constantly called upon to pay far more than his share, or to settle bills about the length of which he remonstrated in vain. He was ill able to afford these ex-penses; for, in addition to his present outlay, there was the prospect of a greater call upon him. Captain Esher had caused law-proceedings to be instituted against the owner of the chemical works upon the river-banks, on the ground that the noxious fumes from the chimneys had greatly injured, and would still more injure, the wood upon his estate. Max maintained that the injuries done to the trees had been inflicted before he came into possession of the works; but certainly the trees were very black and lifeless, and his chemical products were very poisonous, and he had an inner conviction that the day would go against him. Ten thousand pounds was the enormous sum that Esher's solicitors demanded, and, though it was not likely that Max would have to pay so much, he was none the less fearful about the result. A third of that amount would cripple his business; a loss of seven or eight thousand pounds would force him to throw up the whole concern. But he did not think things had come to a

desperate pass. He wanted to fight the
lawyers fairly, and he had the stimulus to the
conflict given by a consciousness of personal
animus. Esher was not only anxious to repair
the damage done to his estate; he wanted to
ruin a man who had insulted him. For this
result he would fight, by fair means or foul,
every inch of the contested ground. On this
account Max put far more spirit, as well as far
more anxiety, into his combat with Captain
Esher's lawyers than otherwise he might have
done.

He saw little of Magdalen Lingard at this
period, but he was more and more attracted
and yet saddened each time he saw her, by
the patient reticence with which she bore the
separation from Daisy and Dolly. Courage
and fortitude were two qualities that he
specially valued in man or woman; and
Magdalen was brave and strong beyond the
conceptions of most people. And yet she
never failed in tenderness for others, except

for him.   He had seen less of her than ever
since the day when she refused him ; and at
times he was disposed to sigh to himself in the
words of Ladislaw's song—

> " Oh me, oh me, what frugal cheer
>   My love doth feed upon !
>   A touch, a ray, that is not here,
>   A shadow that is gone."

Yet in spite of the frugal cheer on which it
lived, his love flourished and grew apace.

Mrs. Cecil Brendon was sitting in an undig-
nified attitude on the nursery floor, at play
with her little girl. "Baby" was an inex-
haustible fund of amusement : she was always
doing something sufficiently novel and striking
to redeem her mother's life from any chance of
monotony.   She was a particularly joyous
little thing, more like the Chaloners than the
Brendons.   She was inclined to be short and
chubby : she had dancing blue eyes, golden
curls, limbs that never rested for five minutes

at a time (as long as she was awake), and a
tongue that jabbered all day long. How
delightful it was to Lenore to feel the warm,
clasping arms and somewhat moist kisses, to
bark like a dog and mew like a cat for Baby's
pleasure, to sing or play or dance for Baby's
benefit half through the day, can only be
understood by happy mothers like herself.
The appearance of new pearly teeth, the
acquisition of novel and extraordinary words,
the saucy defiance of authority and uncompre-
hending want of any kind of fear, afforded
matter of interest and occupation to Lenore
from morning until night. She had already
been seen to arm herself with several works on
education for the better training of the infant
mind; and she kept a volume of English
history on hand because she did not want to
be "quite too ignorant to teach Baby when
she grew older."

Mrs. Brendon grumbled that the child ought
to be called by its proper name, now that it

was a year and seven months old, but father
and mother found it hard to abandon the title
of " Baby " for the stately name, Cecilia, which
she had received. " Cissy " was now and then
attempted, but Baby had evidently great
difficulty in understanding that she could be
addressed by it.

"Oh, Baby, Baby, what have you done to
my hair?" cried Lenore at last, putting up
her hand to the brown tresses that were
certainly very much out of order. " And
there is papa coming : what will he say?"

Cecil's step was heard on the stairs, and
next moment he appeared at the door.

" I thought I should find you here," he said,
smiling at the pretty picture presented by the
mother and her child, "so I came to find you.
Baby-worship going on?"

"Come and worship too," said Lenore.
" I must stay until nurse comes up from tea.
Do you want me? Shall I ring for her?"

"No, I'll come in." And Cecil entered

with an air of not being at home in that
unfamiliar place, the nursery. " I wanted to
ask what you meant to do about Mrs. Dering's
invitation."

" I declined," said Lenore, opening her eyes.

" I wish you would not decline invitations
so often."

" Cecil, dear, this is the first I have declined
since I was able to leave Baby for so long, and
I thought you did not like my going to Mrs.
Derings ? "

" I don't like the woman herself, but everybody goes there. I have been asked two or
three times whether we were going."

" You can go," said his wife, after a little
pause. " I declined only for myself, you
know."

" But I like to have you with me."

" How kind of you," said Lenore, taking
hold of his hand rather mischievously. " But
you must do without me sometimes."

Cecil did not smile, as she expected. He

looked a little bored, walked to the window, and glanced out, then came back to the hearthrug. These movements were signs to Lenore that his mind was uneasy.

"Have you any special reason for wanting me to go on Thursday, Cecil? I daresay I could arrange it with Mrs. Dering."

"No: don't make a fuss, of all things. But another time I think you might ask *me* before you refuse an invitation."

"I will, dear, another time," said Lenore, wondering inwardly what had displeased him in the refusal that they had long ago agreed to send. But she did not care to pursue the subject, and he left the room after saying a few words to Baby.

They did not speak of it again until Thursday evening, when Cecil went alone to the dinner-party that Mrs. Dering gave for her newly-married son on his return from his wedding-tour. The Derings, father and son, were rich soap-boilers; people decidedly below the

Brendons in the social scale, but enormously wealthy. Cecil generally avoided them, and ridiculed their pretensions to refinement; so Lenore had some right to feel surprised at his wanting her to accept their invitation to dinner, even if he chose to accept it for himself.

He came home earlier than she had expected him—before eleven o'clock. She was sitting in the drawing-room, half-asleep over a novel, when he appeared.

"So soon, Cecil, dear? It wasn't a nice party, then?"

"Not particularly." He went to the fire, and stood with his arm upon the mantelpiece, in an abstracted manner. He was generally so full of talk about the people he had seen and the news that he had heard that this silence puzzled Lenore and woke her up. She asked in a much more lively tone,

"Who was there?"

He mentioned the names of two or three persons whom she knew.

"Oh, I should have thought that they would make a pleasant party. Then what went wrong, darling?"

She did not imagine to herself that Cecil's thoughts were running round and round in a sort of rhythmical refrain, "Shall I tell her? Shall I not?" Or again, "Shall I be silent? Shall I speak?" At her question he took down his arm and turned a little, so as to look into the red coals. It was better to tell after all.

"There was a visitor whom I did not much care to see," he said. "Mrs. Dering does not understand Scarsfield society very well. She had asked Miss Roslyn."

He waited for a response. None came for the space of some two minutes. If he had looked round he would have seen that Lenore's face changed colour more than once; that her eyes first opened wide, then fixed themselves upon the floor. At last she uttered a soft, nervous little laugh, and said,

" Well?"

" Well!" repeated Cecil, more boldly and with some indignation. "Can you not see that it was excessively awkward?"

"Yes, it was awkward," she said, slowly. Then she left her seat and came round to him, touching his coat-sleeve with one hand. "You don't think that I mind your having seen her—spoken to her even—again, Cecil? You look half-afraid to tell me about it. I don't mean to be vexed—I should be ashamed to be jealous—when I know that you love me so truly. Of course, you could not help meeting her. I am afraid it was worse for her."

"I don't know that," he answered, astonished at a generosity which he hardly understood, and thinking that she underrated the perils of the situation. "She seemed quite unconscious of anything unpleasant. It was very disagreeable for me."

"Yes. If you could have avoided meeting

her it would have been pleasanter. But it is no use to attract attention by being uncivil. Very few people knew that you were engaged to Miss Roslyn. I am very sorry for you, dear; but I suppose we must expect such meetings if we live in Scarsfield."

"You don't mean to say that we are forced to be acquainted with the Roslyn family?"

"No. When we can quietly avoid them, let us do so; but don't let us set people talking and asking why we quarrelled with them. We used to know them very well, and of course they have been so long abroad that people do not recognise the fact that we are no longer on visiting terms. Perhaps you can manage not to meet her again."

"You take it very coolly," said Cecil. "I thought that you would so much dislike my seeing her!"

"Dear Cecil," she said, earnestly, "I am your wife!"

"You are not like other women," he said,

putting his arm round her. "Some wives would be jealous, you know!" He laughed as he spoke, but there was a little anxiety in his tone.

"The faith that I have in you, Cecil, makes me able to trust you anywhere with anybody. I never feel jealous ; no, not one bit!"

She spoke eagerly, and the bright tears glittered for a moment in her eyes. Cecil stooped to kiss them away, a little touched by her confidence in him. His nature had nobleness enough to wish to respond to it, but perhaps he would have been more content at that moment with a lower and more exacting kind of love ; it would have better suited his own, which craved for as much in return as it gave.

"You are a perfect wife, Lenore," he said, remorsefully, "and I am not half good enough for you."

"Not good enough ? Why not ? You are all that I want when you talk to me and pet in this way. You must not think that I do not prefer your being with me to talking to other people, you know, Cecil; I don't mind your being with them, but I like you best to stay with me."

"Ah! just that touch of womanliness at the end prevents your being too angelic," laughed Cecil, with an air of relief. "You can bear to acknowledge then that you selfishly prefer my devoting myself to you rather than to anybody else?"

"Of course I can," she answered, with a pretty smile and blush. "I am selfish, if I am not jealous, and you always tell me I married into a very selfish family."

He kept his arm round her, and continued to look at her with an air of possession, while she went on more hesitatingly,

"Did Miss Roslyn show that she was vexed at meeting you, Cecil?"

"I don't think she showed any particular kind of feeling."

"I wonder if she knew that you would be there?"

To this Cecil returned no answer.

"You had no idea *she* would be there, of course."

As he was still silent, she raised her face and looked at him. The colour had mounted to his forehead, and he seemed as if he did not know what to say.

"Did you know you were going to meet her?" asked Lenore, withdrawing herself a little from his embrace.

"You are jealous after all," said Cecil, trying to smile.

"No, not jealous, Cecil; but do you think you ought to have gone if you knew——"

"You would not go with me, remember," he said, sulkily throwing himself into a chair. "Besides, I was not sure, I had merely a suspicion——"

"It was not right," she said. But while he looked vexed and gloomy, she added, "However, you will not be likely to see her again, I suppose. I beg your pardon, Cecil ; I did not mean to show any distrust of you. Do as you like about Miss Roslyn—and everything else."

She moved away as she spoke, trying to repress the feeling that her husband had not treated her quite openly in the matter. They did not recover complete cordiality of manner to each other until next day ; for as there had been no quarrel, there could be no re-conciliation, and Cecil was vaguely conscious that his wife thought that her perfect trust had not been quite deserved. He felt guilty enough to be anxious that she should forgive him, but did not care to reopen the subject. So through the following day or two he made a point of paying her great attention, of waiting upon her with a graceful deference which reminded Lenore of the earlier days of their married life. The silent little court-ship touched her; she had never been able to hold out against Cecil's dark eyes and readi-ness to own himself in the wrong. In another day she was too happy in Cecil's love to trouble herself concerning Ruby Roslyn.

END OF VOL. II.